Diary of a Kiwi Kid

By Robin Lee-Robinson

Reviews

Lee Murray - 5 Stars
It is laugh-out loud funny. The writing is spot on, naïve and often chaotic, Robinson perfectly captures the voice of her young protagonist, and some of the malapropisms Rosalyn coins will have readers rolling in laughter. Robinson addresses important issues such as identity, sexuality, social responsibility, and alcohol abuse—albeit seen from Rosalyn's limited nine-year-old understanding, making this an excellent 'shared read' for parents to read aloud to children. Diary of A Kiwi Kid is an excellent memoir, which will resonate for many of us.

Piper Mejir - 5 Stars
Robin Lee-Robinson's forthright protagonist Rosalyn reminds us of our own battles with too much responsibility, too little respect and the crisis of identity that we all faced in homes of busy parents with troubles of their own. However, the novel does leave the reader wondering about the importance of Rosalyn's disappearance and why Jack needed to read her diary.

Nick Adams - 5 Stars
Once I started to follow Roz's diary, I found this a hard book to put own, reading some of it in the bath tub. I suspect a follow-up book, or perhaps a series may (or should be) in the works, as I am interested to find out more about Roz's mysterious disappearance and am eager to read more.

Books By Robin Lee-Robinson

Book 1 - Diary of a Kiwi Kid

Book 2 - Journal of a Junior Writer

Book 3 - Trials & Tribulations of a Trouble Teen

Salting the Gravy

Talkback Toast

Dedication

I dedicate this book to
our children's children's children.

GLOSSARY OF MĀORI WORDS & PHRASES

Ko Jack Jondell ahau. E te kau ma wha oku tau.

My name is Jack Jondell. I am fourteen years old.

Ko Jac Jondell toku ingoa.

My name is Jack Jondell.

hāngī - *earth oven used to cook food with steam from heated* stones.

hapū - *pregnant.*

iwi - *tribal affiliation.*

kapa haka - *cultural performance by a group, e.g. a school group.*

kōhanga reo - *or Te Kōhanga Reo; a preschool education centre where the children speak te Reo.*

kōrero - *talk, discussion; also a story or tale.*

koro - *elderly man, grandfather; a term of respect.*

korowai - *ceremonial cloak ornamented with feathers and twisted tags or hanging threads.*

kuia - *elderly woman, grandmother; a term of respect when speaking to an older woman.*

mahi - *to work, do, perform or make.*

marae - *a collection of buildings for community gatherings.*

mihi - *to greet, acknowledge or thank, etc.*

pākehā - *a person of mainly European descent.*

paua - *large edible abalone (mollusc)*

pēpēa - *baby.*

pikopik - *tender & edible fern shoots.*

tamariki - *children, grandchildren.*

tangi - *funeral, or weeping.*

taonga - *valued possessions, a treasure.*

te Reo - *the Māori language.*

toe toe - *tall grasses with feathery fronds.*

wāhine - *woman or women.*

whaea - *mother or sometimes aunt.*

whakapapa - *your line of descent, or to recite it.*

whanau - *immediate or extended family.*

whāngai - *to feed, nourish, foster or adopt.*

whare - *house, dwelling, building.*

whare nui - *literally a big house, usually a building on the marae.*

Introduction

Jack Jondell seems like your typical Year 10 student, hanging out in Gisborne with his mates. But Jack also writes winning speeches in English and Te Reo, while his twin sister Hinemarama writes rap.

Did they inherit this talent for words from Grandma Rosalyn, who was always determined to be published? She joined Junior Writers while still in primary school. He can't ask her how she did it, because Rosalyn mysteriously disappeared in Bangladesh when she was eighteen. She hasn't been heard of since.

It isn't until 2017, forty years later, that Jack gets a chance to understand what sort of person his grandmother was. Sworn to secrecy, he's handed Rosalyn's diary from her locked writing desk. Other mysteries are hinted at as he reads on, firing Jack with the determination to find out more. Especially, what happened to Rosalyn...

Diary of a Kiwi Kid

JACK JONDELL
GISBORNE, 2017

This afternoon Nan Helene handed me two things. A key on an old shoelace and a little handmade box. When I unlocked it, there was this new USB in a vacuum sealed pack.

I look at her and I go, "I've got heaps already, but thanks."

"Jack, this is different. This flashdrive is your secret diary."

Flashdrive? Secret? My laptop has a password so you can't get into my system anyway, but Nan's 79 so she probably forgot that part.

Earlier in the day this random lady called Jennifer Sorren turned up in a ute with Gisborne Poultry Fanciers Association written across it. She was picking up Nan Helene to take her into town for lunch.

When they returned, she asked me, "Would you like some bantam hens?"

Nah, I don't think so. They're too small for eating, too many tiny bones. Like those quail rich as people eat. Besides we've got heaps of chicken in our freezers. Shut the door! Nan hangs out with some real weird people.

I said, "No, thanks," politely, as I've been taught and after they said their goodbyes and Nan went inside, I got out my laptop and dragged a bean bag under the three jacaranda trees, plugged in Nan's new USB and headed up a new file.

This is my first entry.

SATURDAY

Ko Jack Jondell ahau. E te kau ma wha oku tau.

That's enough. Always start with a bit of a mihi, Uncle Hone says. Protocol. I'm Jack Jondell, and I'm fourteen. I have a twin sister Hinemarama, or Hine for short. Our mother was raised by our grandmother. Well, Nan Helene isn't really our grandmother. Not even!

She's the aunt of our maternal grandmother Rosalyn. Nan Helene and Nanny Sarah have been together like forever, but they've got no tamariki. Apart from Mum, that is.

We all live in Nan Helene's 2-bedroom whare on her half acre section in Kaiti. It's small, but works well for us five because there's a big self-contained sleepout on the property as well. Ours.

There's a mystery in our family concerning our maternal grandmother, Rosalyn Jondell. So much we don't know. Our mother doesn't even remember her biological mother. When Mum was a toddler, Rosalyn disappeared in Bangladesh at the age of eighteen, and has never been seen or heard of since.

So I'll start at the beginning. Grandma Rosalyn had our mother to this dude called Matt Branson when they were like sixteen. Rosalyn and Matt went to primary school together in Elgin, Gisborne. He's one of those wealthy as accountants. Even when he was a little kid everyone knew Matt Branson was going to be good with money. You don't want to start him talking about finance, stocks and shares or the exchange rate.

Don't like to dis our Papa Matt, but he's boring as, so Pākehā you'd never know there's any Māori in him, but there is. He doesn't celebrate his Māori side., knows hardly any Te Reo. But he's always supported us, even though he's been married now for years and has other kids. He's good like that, and Mum is glad she has some half-brothers and a sister through her father, so Hine and I have heaps of cuzzies on that side, too.

When Mum was born everyone was like, that can't be Matt Branson's kid cos the baby looks so Māori and Rosalyn fully Pākehā and Matt's such a white dude.

I overheard Nanny Sarah describe both Matt and Mum as throwbacks. It's all right for the old people to use this racist language, but we'd get in trouble at school if we said half the politically incorrect stuff they do.

They say Rosalyn and Matt were tight. They were going to have this big as wedding on Waikanae Beach when they were twenty. Those plans came to nothing when she disappeared and Papa Matt eventually got together with someone else.

Anyway, Mum and Papa Matt did the DNA test thing about ten years ago. Definitely father and daughter.

The Jondells, including Nan Helene, and Nanny Sarah, they're all Pākehā, but Mum and Hine and me whakapapa back to both Ngati Paroa through Papa Matt.

As well as Ngati Paroa, Hine and me also whakapapa back to Whakatohea and Tuhoe through our own father. Useless bugger, Mum calls our father PK I wish she wouldn't dis him like that, but it's their stuff. Not our business.

Because of Nan Helene's strict rules our father's not allowed to visit when he's stoned or pissed, which is most of the time. Our Mum agrees with her Mum. That's what she calls our Nan. She says we have a duty of care to provide a safe environment for our tamariki and our kuia.

Not that she'd dare refer to Helene and Sarah as old people, anyway, not to their face. Duty of care? Mum let's that Iwi Services mission statement talk take her over a lot. She's worked there like forever.

Hine and I don't see that much of our Dad PK, but he's OK His whānau and us, we're cool. Safe as.

Nan Helene says Māori kids, especially Whakatohea, are 'renowned for writing excellent family history, because they have well-developed whānau connections.'

She keeps talking about that Opotiki girl who got sent to Gallipoli for the First World War centenary for that speech she won. She's so proud of me winning our regional secondary schools speech contest. I delivered in both Te Reo and English.

Nan Helene even reckons Hine's talent for writing and performing rap runs through our bloodline through our grandmother Rosalyn. I'm not too sure about that. Did this cool as genre even exist when Rosalyn was around? Doubt it. I know Nan isn't into rap, even though she pretends to tolerate it. Nan Helene's into old as sounds from the 70s, 80s and 90s.

It was Nan who got Mum into Gisborne Young Writers when she was young, and Hine and me when we were about eleven, though Hine doesn't go any more. That's three generations, and it all started with Rosalyn.

Lots of writers and others around here still remember Rosalyn. There's this lady called Kirsty O'Neil who comes over to see our Nan. She went to school with both Rosalyn and Papa Matt.

Mum has no time for Nan's 'Rosalyn talk' as she calls it. She goes, "My biological mother dumped me on Mum Helene and Mummy Sarah when I was a baby. She's probably still alive and well in Bangladesh, hooked up with some rich as maharajah."

She's always saying how Rosalyn did her a favour, and how she was lucky to be raised by strong wahine in a stable, loving gay marriage. That she has not one but two whaea, plus the support of her biological father.

Once I overheard Nan say to her older sister, our Great-aunt Julie that our Mum is 'scarred and emotionally wounded by a chronically-fractured maternal bond, but she's resistant to counselling.'

There sure is a lot of female kōrero and energy around here. When it gets too much for me, Papa Matt tells me I can bike over to Elgin and chill with him. I hang out often with my great-grandparents, too. Great-grandpa Steve, Nan's little brother. Little! He's like seventy-two.

He lets me carve Māori designs from log offcuts in his mean as shed, giving me the exact same Health and Safety Induction every time, then makes me wear earmuffs and safety glasses. Inside his shed, the walls are covered in A4-laminated photos of him and Rosalyn making a trolley and other stuff. Man, you'd never think it was him in those photos. He looked so different when he had hair, like his boys Josh and Justin.

Josh owns their house now cos they spent so much on airfares to Bangladesh looking for Rosalyn. Josh went with them one time and they got an interpreter to speak with the villagers. Still nothing. Gone without trace.

I'm sorry for them. Mum says Rosalyn ruined them. You can't talk sense to her when it's about her own mother. She says what Rosalyn did in abandoning her is no excuse. She knows all about being a young single mother, and had not one but two pēpē when she was only seventeen herself.

Our place is cool as. It's on a massive section with

all these secluded garden rooms Nan and Rosalyn made from tall hedges and driftwood archways that Nanny Sarah under-planted with roses and exotic vines and stuff. I doubt they could do that mahi now. She makes Hine and me trim the lower branches and prune and mow and dig in compost.

We should be on a garden makeover show to teach people how to do it.

We can have all our friends over at the same time. Mum and her lot can smoke and kōrero hard out or do their women's group buzz at one end. Fence hedges cut down the sound a fair bit and give us heaps of privacy. My sister and our friends can rap and play our sounds outside even in winter cos Nan and Rosalyn made all these cool nova-light, roofed-over gazebos trailing grape and passionfruit vines and each shelter has its own fire brazier.

Nan doesn't approve of sitting around guzzling too many beers, and she and Mum had to come to a bit of an agreement on that. The old people keep away from gangsta rap or drinking anyway. They prefer chilling up at the whare.

Rosalyn also built this cool-as tree house when she was only thirteen, so well-made it ticks all the Health and Safety boxes. I was sure Great-grandpa Steve must have helped her, but Nan says no. He installed the heavy structural support poles and cables, but the rest is all Rosalyn's work. Awesome. Me and Hine sometimes take our foam mattresses up there to sleep out on hot summer nights.

Though our whare itself is small, it's home for Nan, Nanny Sarah, Mum, Hine and me. Years ago when our Mum was at Kōhanga Reo, Papa Matt wanted to set them up with a much bigger house on a tidy section. As if!

Then some developers tried to tell Nan she didn't need so much land and offered heaps of money to sub-divide and told her the house could be extended once the sleepout's gone. Shut up! They haven't been back.

Nan will never sell, and we love that sleepout with its mini-kitchen, toilet and shower. Mum's pleased to have the bedroom area to herself since Papa Matt bought Hine and me a retro caravan each for our eleventh birthday and had them set on blocks. It's like tiny house nation here now. Primo.

We've sold our old bunk set and the room divider. It sure was getting a bit cramped. Papa Matt goes to us like, "You guys need your own space now and Baby-girl shouldn't be sharing a sleepout with a pair of boisterous pre-teens.

Mum's 33 next birthday and he still calls his daughter Baby-girl!!

Nan Helene tells us off about saying she goes, he goes.

"The word said is disappearing from everyday usage."

Why does she worry about dumb as stuff like that?

The caravans are real cool, especially since we re-painted them with graffiti. What's a bummer is we can't sneak our friends over the tin fence any more. Once the caravans arrived, the gardens around them were replanted after the trailer munted the backyard

Nan Helene also extended the height of our corrugated iron perimeter fence and then planted mean as cactus around the inside. Man, that cactus is big now!

We have this coded automatic front gate. Nan let Papa Matt pay for that and it does keep out random callers like the Mormons or door-to-door-sellers. No one gets in or out of our property without the Nans knowing.

For our thirteenth birthday, Papa Matt bought us each a lockable garden shed when he saw Hine's clothes poking out Mum's wardrobe. Mine's stuffed with my surfboard and my wheels.

I think Papa Matt still misses Rosalyn. He says she was a creative and talented girl, and never boring. I googled her pen names Roz Jondell and Ross Bovary and found published works under both. But when she was hapu Nan Helene and Sarah agreed to whangai the baby, so they all lived together.

Some time after the baby was born, Rosalyn, who was real fluent in Te Reo for a Pākehā, got this opportunity to travel to Bangladesh with Māori Television to cover stories about child labour in clothing factories. That had been a long-term goal apparently and she'd pitched them the idea and wrote the script.

Rhamat of Bangladesh, her children's book, sold well both here and over there. Rosalyn drove the truck and was handy on film and was a natural in front of the camera. Everyone says Rosalyn had the potential to be the ultimate Jack or Jill of many trades. She had other schemes and trips lined up.

We still don't know what happened. Rosalyn went back into this slum by herself after a shoot day was over. No-one knows why and everyone agrees it was a dumb thing to do. All this happened over thirty years ago. Over there, the case is closed. There's no leads or any hard evidence of foul play. Bangladesh police are lame, IMO. I want to go on Lost and Found, the missing persons show and find out what did happen to her.

What if she's still alive? Rosalyn is 49 now, the same as Papa Matt, Ms Sorren and that random Kirsty lady who visits Nan every so often.

SUNDAY

When I ran into the kitchen this morning I nearly tripped

over Nanny Sarah's walker where she'd left it by the door. Her mobility scooter was missing from the porch. She'll be down at the church and gone half the day.

Nanny Sarah is eighty-two, three years older than Nan Helene. I heard the iwi work van start up about 6.30am. Mum had to leave real early to help out at the marae for a tangi of one of the old kuia. She'll be sleeping among the snorers in the whare nui tonight.

Hine might hang out there too with our cousins if there's enough room. She's still at her bestie's place in Te Hapara now. Bet Aunty Erena will make Hine do the ginger puddings for the tangi. Nan will text them both later. Nan's so cool. She's kept up with technology and Facebooks heaps, not like my friends' koro and kuia I know. Useless as with devices!

As soon as everyone was out Nan Helene went to show me something. She leads me into the spare room and points to this writing desk that's been there like forever.

"Therein lie secrets you may wish to unravel some day, Jack."

That's Nan Helene for you. Being all mysterious.

Later I go to her, "Nan, I can't think of anything else but what's in there. I just have to know."

She crooked her arthritic pinkie finger around mine and swore me to secrecy.

"Until tomorrow, Jack. Then all will be revealed."

MONDAY

I dreamed about Grandma Rosalyn last night. I was walking through this slum in Bangladesh and she was filming me. I go to introduce myself to her and begin, "Ko Jack Jondell toku ingoa..." when she interrupts my mihi.

"I know who you are, Sam-I-am. You're my grandson Hamiora." (That's the Māori name for Sam.)

"That's impossible," I tell her. "You're eighteen and Hine and me are fourteen."

When I woke up it was as if I'd met my real grandmother for the first time. I don't use my given name much and not many people know it. I call myself Jack. No one calls me Sam either, not anymore. Then I remembered that 'Sam-I-am' is in this Green Eggs and Ham book with Rosalyn's name on it.

Our Great-grandmother Esmé used to read it to us when we stayed overnight with her when were little. Random as.

Even though it's out of zone, Hine and I go to Langbourne High School because we're twins and it's co-ed. We're Year 10. The only other state school alternative is Garrett Boys and Girls High Schools. I took my bike today so I can sneak back to the house.

Told Hine I'm getting fit and working off my coke and McDonalds diet. She won't even notice, but if she says anything about not seeing me at school then I know that the Year 9 kapa haka group are going to the district inter-schools rehearsals today. I'll say I went with them to do lights and sound.

If Mum finds out I cut class she'll go mental cos of NCEA, the big deal exam. Nan Helene wrote a note explaining I had a doctor's appointment and needed to be excused from morning break for the rest of the day.

She goes, "Some things are much more important than school lessons, Jack."

I biked back to the house to find we had the place to ourselves as Nan had planned. Hine had left on the school bus. Nanny Sarah had been picked up earlier by the Sunshine Community van and gone to some old people's function in Tolaga Bay and Mum was at work.

In the fridge was some left-over raw fish Mum had made for the tangi and our kitchen was full of that fresh frybread smell. The Nannies were welcome to that. I got out Hine's ginger pudding and the cream. She won't mind I had some. It was good. Nan Helene growled me to save some for my sister and mother.

After I'd washed the dishes, we had to do Nan Helene's pinkie promise thing again and then we walked into the room that had been Mum's when she was little. For years there's been no furniture like bed or TV. Nothing but the old writing desk, a coffee table and bookcase, a comfy chair, bean bags and foam mattresses stacked against the wall.

Marae-style sleepovers. Nan's funny. If old people stay she makes me vacuum first and pile up the mattresses five high. She calls it the quiet room and likes us to read in there without 'electronic distractions.'

Mum says she's never seen that writing desk open. I always knew there was something special in there. I figured it must be a korowai or some ancient bone carving necklace kept for when we graduate or something.

"You stay there," she ordered.

She had a key in her hand and unlocked the desk, then passed over a pair of gloves.

"Put them on."

I did, and she handed me this old as journal and told me I could read a little bit each day when no one else was around.

"You're not allowed to leave the room with it. No talking about it to anyone but me. Any secrets you uncover about others are sacred."

Other instructions, too. Leave your mobile on the kitchen table. You're not allowed to copy anything down.

No eating or drinking while you're reading it.

"Jack, I'll lock this taonga up each time and only I know where the key is hidden. If anything happens to me, it's in my will that Kirsty O'Neil is to take possession of the desk and its contents until you reach your majority."

What? That Kirsty lady's not even whānau. Oh, whatever! I was shaking with anticipation. It had to be some mean as kōrero in that old journal to be locked up for so long.

As soon as Nan Helene left, I dragged over a bean bag and started reading.

OMG, 1977!!!

That was 40 years ago

ROSALYN JONDELL
GISBORNE, 1977

SATURDAY

I went with my Aunt Helene to the church gala in Kaiti, Gisborne. And she bought me this journal off a stall. It's old fashioned, with a padlock. and a key was taped to the cover. I used Dad's CRC when he wasn't looking to free up the lock. The olds won't even know I've got it, just Aunt Helene, so it's going to be a secret diary after all.

Two pages had already been torn out. Another had weird stuff written in pencil, Bonnie wee lad 9lb 12oz and a list, Glaxo 6oz and 5oz. Oz? What does that mean? I ripped that out, too. Then I pulled a shoelace out of an old pair of sneakers Dad had in the rubbish pile and threaded it through. That key is *never* coming off my neck.

Auntie is always buying me things. I think I'm her favourite, although she says she loves all three of us equally. Yeah, right!

A lot of writers kept journals before they become famous. I think that's why she bought it. I overheard her telling the olds I have untapped potential.

There was this pretend gypsy caravan at the gala, and a woman inside wearing colourful scarves and bells and bangles. The sign outside said 'Madame Bovary. Fortune-Teller, and I thought it'd be great if she could tell me when I'm going to be famous.

I was supposed to stay in full sight of Auntie, but Madame Bovary got me to cross her palm with silver and come into her parlour. It was nothing but a decorated truck, and I only had two 50 cent coins left.

Grey smoke filled the parlour from long burning sticks. She told me I was a special child with an extraordinary gift and a confused identity. I was destined for future wealth and popularity.

My reading was never finished because my aunt appeared with duck eggs, a bunch of radish and home-made fudge poking out of her bags. She marched in and dragged me off the chair. So embarrassing. Then she started screaming at the woman not to pray on a naïve child. She had a point about naïve children, I suppose, because Charlie Davis was next in the queue. He's this big boy repeating Year 5 again.

I told my aunt there was no praying going on. Aunt Helene was yelling "Charlatan!" and "Madame Bovary? That's a bogus name if ever I heard one" and "My big rear end." That was funny because Auntie is skinny as.

"Confused identity?" she shouted. "You unprincipled shark. Why, it's as clear as the nose on my face that my niece is a confounded tomboy."

Then she marched me away in front of a gathering crowd after threating to expose the woman for smoking drugs in front of minors. I'm sure Madame Bovary would have confirmed my talents if my aunt hadn't turned up right then. That's a word I haven't yet looked up charlatan.

Aunt Helene is good for my vocabulary because instead of swearing she uses descriptive words. Even the teachers say I have an extremely rich vocabulary for my age. I must have learnt confounded from Auntie when I was still in nappies.

When I asked her why she didn't want the woman

praying for me, she laughed, and explained the difference between praying for and preying on.

SUNDAY

Confounded sports on TV. Couldn't get Dad off the couch. England versus Wales, or something as mind-numbingly dumb. So we didn't end up going to the beach and fighting over ice-creams after all. Tried to talk Mum into taking us, but she wanted a day to chill.

When we do go, they like to sit in the car watching us playing, the olds. She gave me money instead.

Guilt money. I know when we're being neglected. I went for a walk to the shops on my own. At least there was no push-me pull-me little brothers dropping lollies on the ground and trying to put them back with the dirt still on them.

I'm taking them to school as well now they're five. My school, worse luck.

MONDAY

Boring school day. Boring, that is, until Melissa O'Brien wet herself. Mr Morrissey went to the caretaker's shed for a bucket and mop. No one offered to help. Melissa was crying so hard she got sent home. Serves him right that he had to mop up the puddle himself.

Melissa asked to be excused three times. Mr Morrissey looked at his watch. He made her wait for the morning break. That will teach him.

I asked to be excused straight after that and he said yes. Then I said, "No, I think I can wait, Mr Morrissey," hopping from one foot to the other. He said in a gruff voice, "You are excused."

"No, but," I began, and that's when he shouted at me, "Go now. And hurry."

Mr Morrissey should retire from teaching if he can't cope with the stress.

TUESDAY

Dad was in a bad mood this morning because his alarm didn't go off. Groaned about being late for some big job at the factory across the Old Colonial Bridge that the old homeless man lives under. He had to pick up two guys in the work van. "The pipes were compromised," he muttered, and something about the S-bends.

He ruffled Josh's hair as he went out the door.

"Take my advice, boy. Don't be a plumber."

"Might be one myself," I said. "Plumbing can make you big money, I've heard."

Dad raised his eyebrows and gave me this strange look.

WEDNESDAY

We had a power cut at the school today and the lights in the classroom went out. Four-Eyes Logan Sinclair couldn't properly see the teacher's writing on the board and today over half the class couldn't either, so we all got sent outside to play.

The other classes must've had same problem as there were heaps of kids outside. I heard Mrs Girton moaning to Mr Morrissey about electrical services as they walked into the staffroom. The confounded Poverty Bay Electric Power Board and their power cuts.

The teachers couldn't even boil the jug for morning tea and were grumpy for the rest of the day.

THURSDAY

Thursday is Mum's payday and she always brings us home a jelly-tip ice block. Yep. She did.

FRIDAY

Maths test. Ryan Garrett did that thing where he pretends he has to go to the toilet. He always does. Mr Morrissey said, "I'll give you the benefit of the doubt this time, young man."

Then when Ryan had left the room, he added, "We won't start the test until Ryan gets back."

When Ryan returned to find us waiting for him, he pretended to throw up and Mr Morrissey handed him the class bucket. We couldn't stop laughing.

SATURDAY

So glad the weekend is here. Dad put the twins and me on the ten o'clock bus into town. He's always happy waving goodbye. Said he's off with the boys to sink a few, whatever that means.

Mum was waiting for us when the bus stopped outside the Americano where she works. Justin and Josh got covered in tomato sauce playing jet planes with their chips and left their hamburger buns half-eaten after licking off the melted cheese. Justin hates lettuce and Josh beetroot, though they like burger patty itself.

After lunch I cleaned them up and put the buns in a bag before taking the twins to feed the ducks on the river across the road while Mum finished up. At half-past one she brought the car around to collect us. She said all the same things on the way home. About good behaviour, her boss and how lucky we were to afford little extras because of her job. I nearly choked on my Lifesaver sweet because it's me wearing the house key to school.

By that stage the twins were shoving each other in the back seat and yelling. Every Saturday I nearly break my neck sorting out the terrible two to save our family from a major traffic accident. I deserve more pocket money. I told Mum so, but she didn't answer.

SUNDAY

Went around to Lori Merton's place. She's one of ten kids. Every day Lori pegs washing and peels a bucket of spuds, so first, I had to help her with chores. Then ask nicely while she was out of the room, "Please, Mrs Merton, can Lori come over to my house?" (As though it was my idea all along.) When Lori came back, her Mum would cross-examine her.

"Have you done all your chores? Made all the beds?"

"Yes, Mum."

"Changed the baby?" Lori nodded.

"Dishes?" She nods again.

"All right then, but only for an hour."

I'd been seeing items on the news about exploited kids in India. Lori doesn't watch much TV because she's always bathing kids.

When I talk to her, I reckon I'm not the only victim of child exploitation in Elgin, Gisborne, New Zealand, The World.

MONDAY

So boring at school today except when Charlie Davis broke the chair he stood on. He needs to be in a class with bigger furniture. And soon.

TUESDAY

Still nothing much happening in class. I had fun watching Ben Marks during the comprehension test. He either shook his head or nodded before jotting down his answer. What was funnier was watching Lily, Charlie and Sam copying him.

When teacher asked why I wasn't getting on with my

work, I said, "I'm thinking, Mr Morrissey. Do capitalists always come undone when they exploit their poor or ignorant village workers?"

He rolled his eyes at that, and again when I told him I like to keep up with the news of the world. He used that old saying Aunt Helene likes to come out with about teaching grandmothers to suck eggs. I'm so sick of having no-one who appreciates the way I think.

WEDNESDAY

Boring again. We had religious class where this old lady from the church talks mostly about God and the Bible. The teachers are always happy to let the religious instructors get on with it while they drink tea together in the staffroom. After we'd sung Jesus loves the little children, all the children of the world, I asked, "Does Jesus love Rhamat from Bangladesh?"

She stared at me blankly. Yet another grown up who never watches the news! I had to explain that Rhamat is our age and works all day sewing buttons on shirts and doesn't go to school.

THURSDAY

Turns out Madame Bovary was right. I do seem to sense when strange or special things are about to happen. Like today when Mr Morrissey said, "We have a new pupil joining us. Class, say hello to Kirstie Jarrett."

I couldn't stop staring at this new member of our class. She was tall, taller than me, and neat in a Farmers Department Store dress Mum had tried to get me into. I keep telling her I want to dress smart. Kirstie's hair was pulled straight back under a stretchy headband.

(Mum says that's called a bando.)

She'd soon be part of Victoria's gang, I could tell. Mr

Morrissey sent her over to my group desk at the back of the room and asked me to buddy up with Kirstie. Me, of all people! I'd have to get rid of her after showing her around during the break. I prefer my own company.

But by lunchtime she'd grown on me. Besides, she had a bunch of grapes and home-made lemonade in an awesome drinks bottle. I only had a box of raisins and two peanut butter sandwiches.

Kirstie didn't look like a great storyteller, but she was. She told me about an old farm her Dad managed way back in the Gisborne hills, near some historic place Te Kooti had occupied in the 1800s.

"Te who?" I asked, and when she told me, I decided to let her hang about. Apart from me, she was the most interesting kid in school. Besides, she was what Aunt Helene calls stimulating company. By the time the bell rang to end the school day, Kirstie had invited me to come back to her place.

I had to explain I was a house slave, that because my mother works to improve our lives, I don't have normal freedom like regular kids. Every week day I open the house with the key round my neck, fix afternoon tea for the twins, then wait for Mum to come home from work. Sometimes I even have to turn on the stove and start cooking the pot of soaking potatoes she did before breakfast.

"Tea has to be on the table by 5.30," I went on, because Dad's a hard-working plumber. "He's always hungry and he has to have a bath first because he stinks."

Kirstie stared at me sadly. "Later?" she said.

I nodded. Later, if I can."

When Mum finally arrived home. I raced over to find Kirstie sitting on their letterbox. There were unpacked boxes everywhere. She told Jimmy to make us a cold milk Milo. He grinned as he poured in at least a quarter cup of sugar first. He's four years old and ginormously fat.

"He'll get diabetes if he carries on like that," I said.

Then her mother came into the room, saw sugar over the kitchen table and growled at him. He said his sister told him he could. We pretended he was lying and he got sent to his room. Then I noticed the time and had to run all the way home.

Over dinner I couldn't stop talking about Kirstie.

"Kirstie this and Kirstie that," Mum said in a funny voice.

"Sounds like Rosalyn has made a new friend. Eat your mashed potato nicely, Rosalyn dear, stop playing with it."

"Roz," I corrected. "And you don't *make* someone. She's been around for nine years."

I hate that thing where grown-ups make faces when they think you're not looking and I get creeped out every time I hear that stupid name they gave me. Mum told me once I was named after her cousin who died. Thanks, Mum. Then Dad argued my name was from two old maid aunts on his side dating back to the days of the immigrant ship. Rose and Lynne. Parents! I don't know who to believe.

"Rosalyn is a filthy little girl in rags," I said. "A witch's daughter living in a hovel in some ancient forest in merry England. Not a regular nine-year old Kiwi kid like me."

FRIDAY

Had that dream again where Mr Collinson the Principal is drowning and I save him. Everyone cheers, and I become popular and extremely rich like Madam Bovary predicted. Then I wake up.

Yesterday was the best day of my life. I have a best-friend to hang out with. I hope. I picked my navy-blue skirt off the floor. It wasn't too dirty. I only wear pleated skirts with a plain, light-coloured conservative top to school, and if it's cold, one of my jerseys. I don't wear button-up cardigans and I hate twinsets.

My grandmother and my nana both knit. My Dad says our family has enough knitwear to re-sink the Wahine.

I'm not like the other kids in their budget or labelled brands, T-shirts with stuff written on them, or their sweatshirts with logos. They used to tease me, but they've given up on that now because I don't care what they say. I am practising the corporate look I read about in Aunt Helene's magazines. They say fake it till you make it so I dress for success.

I never wear dresses and Mum's given up. She's bought me four plain pleated skirts in dark colours, and another that's light-coloured for best. For school I wear white or pale-coloured shirts. Outside school, I'm a different kid, though. I wear shorts, or one of my collection of op shop jeans, bellbottoms, hipsters and flares. I've got lots of patterned shirts and waistcoats and wide belts.

But I'm lucky if I get to school with everything in order, because Josh nearly pulls one arm out of its socket while Justin dawdles and can never resist running a stick along Mrs Wheeler's tin fence.

Once we've made it across the school zebra crossing, they let go, and my arms spring back and hang there. No wonder Dad says they're too long for my body. I'm like one of those monkeys you used to get in the cereal whose arms you link together.

Mr Collinson droned on and on as usual at assembly. This was the third time this week he's gone on and on about bad men in long black coats offering children confectionary. Warning us not to get into any stranger's car.

Why can't teachers use words all the kids can understand? I looked at the five-year olds and could only see Josh. I think Justin was hiding behind him. Mr Collinson shouldn't scare the little ones.

He cast me a withering glance as I whispered this to Lori. It was a warning, I knew. Next time he'd say, "Eyes to the front, Rosalyn Jondell."

Lucky for him he didn't growl at me or if I dream about him tonight, I'd let him drown.

SATURDAY

Kirstie came by early this morning. Her mother has invited me and the twins over for lunch. Dad said it was too short notice and we got put on the bus as usual. Shame, because I could have fancied spaghetti and meatballs, with crusty bread and a salad.

When we got to the Americano that song April Sun in Cuba by Dragon was playing on the radio and I must have been singing along because one of the customers said you have a nice voice, dearie, and asked if I'm in a church choir!! As if.

I don't see myself as a lead singer now or ever, but when the Rolling Stones magazine interviews some rock group I'll be working for they'll tell the reporter our roadie is indispensable. Lugs sound and lighting equipment around and knows every freeway in Hollywood, L.A. and London and sets everything up for us. Our group couldn't possibly function without Ross Jondell.

"Who's Ross Jondell, dear?" the lady asked and she gave me this funny look. One day she'll be sorry she didn't take me up on my offer to sign the menu on her table.

Mum was serving behind the counter, frowning at me.

She'll have to get used to it when I'm being mobbed by fans, but I know it's hard for parents when their child is in the limelight.

SUNDAY

It's fun having someone to hang out with. I took Kirstie down the railway tracks to the swamp. Her father doesn't have a normal job, she told me. He disappears into the bush and emerges all bloody and covered in possum guts. He's probably as smelly as my own Dad.

He's making the boys a high bed bunk each. He says he's sick to death of them bickering over whose turn it is to have the top bunk every night with a run of the mill bunk set and now each will have a high bunk of their own. Mum says it's a brilliant idea and it makes better use of the room because the other furniture can go underneath.

I'm not letting on, but I'm a bit jealous. And it's going to be harder for me to make two top bunks instead of just one and none of us know when Justin will grow out of wetting the bed.

MONDAY

Kirstie and I nearly had an argument at lunch-time. She reckons the week begins on a Sunday, not on a Monday. I'm more grown-up than Kirstie because I'm three months older so I'll look it up later and prove her wrong.

It all started because of that song: I'll be home on a Monday, somewhere around noon.

"How dumb can you get?" Kirstie said. "Home on a Monday. That could mean any Monday."

I guess you can get away with not making sense when you're a songwriter. It's poetic licence. Artists have a licence too. Anyway, turns out we're both writing diaries. We've agreed to compare notes as we approach old age.

Probably when we're thirty, if we make it that far. I'll leave instructions for Kirstie on where to find mine, in case not. I expect my diary will be valuable by then. Like that girl Anne Frank's we studied in history. I don't know about Kirstie's. I don't want either Josh or Justin reading it. If they can even read by then.

TUESDAY

The story I wrote in class today totally impressed Mr Morrissey. He got me up front to read it. Yes, the lot! He said it contained some wonderful imagery for an attempt by a nine-year old and that it had 'the right pace. He liked the characterisation. I copied that down.

Then he stood there and reminded us about plausibility in story-writing. My hero couldn't pluck his mate one-handed from the choppy sea with the swell and tide as I described it, using only one arm, while the other operated the outboard motor. Only a superhero could achieve that feat.

Obviously, Mr Morrissey doesn't watch films or TV. Superheroes can do anything even in stupid tight underpants or a flapping cape. How are those writers plausible? I ask you!!! And James Bond swinging off a rope under a helicopter by one hand and shooting spies with the other. But you can't argue with teachers.

WEDNESDAY

We had swimming this afternoon with the Senior Class. We marched down two by two in straight lines. More or less! Like Mum's old Madeline picture books she used to read me. One line of boys, one of girls. Except for me, of course. I ran ahead. Besides, neither Mr Morrissey or Mrs Girton look like nuns.

We use the Welston Primary School pool because ours

was demolished a few years back. A new classroom is there now.

One of the big girls in Mrs Girton's class was excused because it was that time of the month. She showed Mrs Girton a note from her mother. Nancy said the same thing, but Mr Morrissey reminded Mrs Girton that Nancy had been excused swimming for that very reason only two weeks ago and they made her get in the pool.

It's weird. What does it matter what day of the month we go swimming? I don't get it.

THURSDAY
The gang we call the Perfect Six were playing ball and pavement games as usual. Kirstie went up to Victoria Allen and asked if we could join in. She stared us up and down and said,

"You can, Kirstie Jarrett, but Rosalyn Jondell can't."

"Why not?" I asked.

"Because..." in that stupid drawn-out drawl of hers," Victoria said.

"She'll be sorry when I'm grown-up and throw an awesome pool party at my Parnell mansion for all the other famous writers and film world people. I will invite everyone from my old neighbourhood except the Perfect Six. If they try and gate-crash security will throw them out.

Later on Valerie Dixon came over to say she was OK about us joining in, she liked us both. Then she hurried away in case Victoria or Catherine or one of the others saw her talking to us. Aunt Helene came for tea. Mum always serves a grown-up menu when she comes. That's fine by me. I take after Aunt Helene, I have sophisticated tastes, too.

Mum made the kids try the recipe she got off

Hudson and Halls: Ginger Marinated Chicken with Wilted Spinach and Red Capsicum. When they spat the first mouthful out, she opened up a tin of baked beans and sausages for them.

Earlier I had to rush to the shops for sesame oil. The 4-Square didn't stock cinnamon quill or star anise and Mr Patel sent me home with Gregg's powdered ginger. He'd run out of fresh.

Mum used tomatoes from our garden, instead of capsicum. Dad couldn't tell the difference and he thought Mum's steamed silverbeet was the wilted spinach. He's no connoisseur like Aunt Helene and me.

Auntie talked all through the lemon tart and crème fraiche dessert about my writing prowess. She said talent like mine needs nurturing. I jotted down prowess to look it up later. Mum took Josh's dessert away when he pushed his plate away, and Justin left his, too. Mum brought them ice cream and when they'd slurped it down, sent them off bed early. Ha ha ha.

The olds rang Mrs Milton next door, then went for a walk after dinner. I stayed home because halfway round the block Mum and Dad start holding hands and being gross, or they dole out safety hints to kids from my school on riding a bike. Or they talk about the mortgage. That's some kind of death hold. Yuk. Don't know why they'd want it.

I told Dad the other day Kirstie's parents have got the right idea. They rent. They don't annoy their kids with talk of council rates. He said, "They're state housing tenants, Rosalyn," as though that's a bad thing.

Tonight their bedroom door was partly open, and they were talking about me. I heard Dad say, "Why not, Esmé? You know what happened to her own kids."

I didn't and I missed the next bit. Dad went on, "Let her take an interest in Rosalyn, who could have more talent than we give her credit for. Where's the harm? It could be the making of her and would certainly, take the pressure off us."

I was confused. Were they going to give me to Aunt Helene? First the Perfect Six rejected me and now Mum and Dad want to give me away. I cried myself to sleep.

FRIDAY

I found Lori settling her little brother in the infant class and took her to the other end of the field where we wouldn't be overheard.

"My parents are giving me away," I told her. I felt Lori should be the first to know. She only lives three doors down from me and we've been friends since long before we started school.

"What? They're sending you to Kaiti to live with your aunt?"

"Not exactly…"

She shrugged. "Either way you've got a bedroom to yourself. There's four in mine. Wish I could go and live with an aunt, one with no kids. I'd love to be an only child."

Sometimes Lori just doesn't get it. She was no use in a crisis of this nature and I went looking for Kirstie.

"I'm miserable," I said, and told her the story.

"Serves you right for ease-dropping," she said.

"What do you mean?" I said. "At least I know they're planning something."

"Planning what? You've only heard part of the conversation."

I walked away. Kirstie was no use either. I'd have to wait and see. It was going to be *agony.*

SATURDAY

When we got back from Mum's work, she asked me to take a bowl of banana custard and some date loaf to the Finches. They live on the one and a quarter acre section backing on to our place.

Mum keeps telling us we must go around the block, not climb the fence, and Dad is always threatening to fix the end of our fence where the Sorrens and I have broken it down over the years.

Jennifer, Isobel and I cut across Finch's paddock to end up in one another's back yards. It saves us walking right around the block. When Isobel and Jennifer Sorren arrive, I ask them not to make the fence squeak, to sneak round our back yard and up our driveway. Mostly it works, but once Dad caught them.

"Where did you two come from? Was just looking down the street. Funny I didn't see you. Now you *do know* you're not allowed to cross the Finch's paddock, don't you? Even though your house is just over there."

He pointed past where our fence is broken. Our footprints have worn down a track. You can see their place clearly because it's a back section. The Sorrens' driveway is off the other street, and really close through our shortcut.

"Mr Finch would have kittens if he caught you climbing over. He likes to keep his fences tidy."

Mr Sorren doesn't give a toss about the state of his fence. Every time I go there, I worry it's about to fall down on me as I scramble over.

Apart from getting in trouble for using the shortcut, the other reason I don't want to go to the Finches is I broke a rung of his old wooden ladder while climbing up onto their clipped bamboo hedge. But I don't think he knows yet. That rickety old ladder still rests where I left it lying against the hedge.

"Take the boys with you," said Mum. "You know how much she loves to see you all."

All of us? Does she? I wanted to say. Does everyone in the world love cute little boy twins. I don't think so. And what does that make me? Just the babysitter bringing them over.

As far as I know, Mrs Finch never gets out of bed. I've never seen her anywhere else.

"Oh, Mum, do I have to? Her bedroom is dark, and it smells. Besides, Justin's scared of her and hides behind Josh."

"Nonsense. The smells are nothing but camphor, disinfectant and lavender. Well, just take Josh then."

In the end, she made us go. I felt like Little Red Riding Hood taking my loaded basket to Grandma in the deep dark forest. Mrs Finch got to be the wolf under the blankets. And Little Red Riding Hood was luckier than me. She got to go alone.

Old Ken Finch has a tummy like a pregnant lady, but Mum didn't need to explain about hernias to the twins every time. No wonder Justin is dramatised. I get sick of hearing the story every time we go there, and we usually get it all over again from Mrs. Finch. But both Mum and Dad keep telling us not to ask about Ken Finch's hernia.

Apparently, in 1958 some surgeon in Poland walked out of a hernia operation he was performing to get some money from the bank across the road. In those days you couldn't get cash after four on a Friday. Anyway, the patient died and that's why her husband won't get his hernia sorted.

"Ken could have an operation tomorrow." Mrs Finch

always speaks as if she's dying. "He never will. He's a stubborn old git."

If she's a sorry invalid like she always says, why isn't she in hospital herself? I had to fluff up her pillows and straighten the candlewick bedspread while Josh sat at the end of her bed trying to finish a stale gingernut and staring at the closed curtain. She was still going on about her husband.

"Hates doctors, does my Ken. Did I ever tell you about the surgeon in Poland? It's because of him, you see."
I couldn't wait to get out of there.

"Come on, Josh. Mum wanted us home early."

Mrs Finch always ends our visit with the same tearful farewell.

"Rosalyn, dear, please bring both the boys next time." She hugged Josh hard. "But I'll say a proper goodbye to this little one now, because this might be the last time you see me."

"Where are you going?" asked Josh before I could shush him. I wondered exactly the same thing at his age, but unlike Josh I was far too polite to ask.

A tear rolled down her cheek and she got out her hanky.

"Oh, my boy. You don't want to know."

Before I hustled Josh away we had to promise to visit again and not to drop the eggs that I'd collected from the chook-house in their paddock.

"And don't forget to come again, and soon, you hear? Do thank your dear mother for the custard and cake. I'll phone to tell her you're headed home."

The minute we reached our porch, I could hear Mum talking. I put my finger over my lips to keep Josh quiet.

Mum put the phone down with a bang, and said to Dad,

"There's nothing wrong with Mrs Finch. She's a hyper-con..." something or other.

"She's been rabbiting on like that for ever, Esmé." He put on a silly voice. "Poor me. I'll soon be gone. This is probably the last time you see me."

Mum giggled. "We must look up that munch house sin drome again, Steve."

Hyper con?

Munch house sin drome?

Justin came round the corner and jumped on us. Mum and Dad saw us sitting on the concrete steps and stopped laughing. I went to my room and found the dictionary.

SUNDAY

I have to be careful because I'm sure I can be seen on top of the Finch's bamboo hedge by neighbours off the other street. Dad told me once, "It's permanently trimmed to about 18 feet in height."

I've been thinking of building a treehouse up there, but there's nothing to nail anything onto. If I ask Dad's advice about fixing tree platforms onto bamboo, he'll guess what I'm up to straight away.

The books on treehouse building in the library are for regular trees. This is a big problem and I blame my parents. They should have thought to plant a tree when they bought the house before they had any kids.

MONDAY

Jennifer's mad at me. She wouldn't even look at me until lunch-time and I've got the desk right next to hers. All because Mrs Finch asked me to collect the eggs. Now Jennifer says the chooks have been put off the lay because I'm a stranger and they don't like my smell.

Isobel, who's ten, only one year older than Jennifer and in the Year 6 Senior Class, said not to worry about it. I didn't know Jennifer got paid good pocket money to take care of Mrs Finch's chooks. Finally sorted and Jennifer and I are friends again. When she looked over the fence and saw me in *her chook-house* on Saturday, she thought the job was being offered to me. I said I'm too busy.

"You're lucky because of all the lawn-mowing you get. In our house Warner and Vinny get first pick of the paid chores and we fight for the ones thy don't want. We're too close in age."

Nine, ten, twelve and thirteen. I never thought of that before. Just put it down to me being over-worked compared to Jennifer and Isobel.

TUESDAY

I bet if Jennifer had to mow a real lawn, she wouldn't be jealous. Mr Diver's lawn-mower's ran out of petrol. His refill can was empty, too. I said I'd fill both at the gas station down by the shops after school.

He gave me $20 and told me to bring back a receipt and the change. I invited Jennifer to come with me and she did, but that's the last time I'm pushing that hunk of tin down the road with its wonky wheel. Least it's ready for mowing when I get a chance.

WEDNESDAY

Yuk. Bible in Schools again today. Got in trouble from Mr Morrissey this morning for talking to Kirstie. I was only asking her to help move that pile of hardboard the caretaker piled up by the incinerator. It's exactly what I need to line the top of the bamboo hedge so I can sit on it and crawl along.

We plan to sneak out at midnight and return to school to get it. I'm wondering what's happening with plans for my move to Kaiti. Still heard nothing.

THURSDAY
Went to bed early so I could meet Kirstie outside at midnight. Problem is, I slept right through and didn't know what I was going to say to Kirstie at school. She would have waited for me outside for ages and I felt bad about that.

Turned out to be Kirstie saying sorry to me. At midnight the dog in the corner house started barking and she had to creep back and climb in through her window before anyone woke up. Ha ha. She still doesn't know I slept in. Ha ha ha. She will do, when she reads this diary.

FRIDAY
It's been over a week since I told Lori I'm probably leaving home. When she asked me about it I had to say still no word. After school Kirstie, the twins and I carried the bigger pieces of the old hardboard home in one load. Mum passed us along the road. When she met up with us in our driveway she said, "Where did you get that? And what are your plans for it?"

"The caretaker was about to burn it in the school incinerator. I've got an idea for lining the laying boxes in the Finch's chook-house."

"Chip off the old block, Rosalyn. Just like your Dad. So kind-hearted with a mind brimming with ideas for Number 8 DIY."
Ha ha ha. If only she knew.

SATURDAY
I'm in luck. I'm invited for tea at Kirstie's and the olds have agreed. Her Mum is doing manuka smoked venison with pikopiko and watercress. Bet they'll serve something like Baked Alaska for dessert.

We only have watercress with bacon bones and potato.

I don't even know what pikopiko is. Mum said we did have venison once. Must have been so long ago I can't remember.

When we got home from her work, my parents had this argument and it wasn't about me this time. She complained that Dad had beer breath and he yelled, "For crying out loud, woman. I have a couple of drinks once a week on a Saturday with my mates. At least you don't have to drag me out of the boozer like some around here we know. Do you hear me whinging when you go out with the girls?"

"All right, Steve," she said, "you've made your point."

He went on, "Remember your Christmas work do two years ago? Don't you recall staggering in at four in the morning?"

"That's enough, Steve," said Mum. Her face was red by now. "Not in front of the children."

"I had to hold your hair back as you puked in the loo, didn't I? Or have you forgotten that fiasco?"

Mum never said another word. When I got back from mowing Mr Diver's lawn Dad was still sulking. I went into his shed to help him build the bunk. I was allowed to use the table-saw under Dad's supervision though I had to listen to a lecture on safety then put on the safety glasses and earmuffs. When I asked him when I can use the table-saw by myself he said, "When you're twenty-five and you've left home, so I don't have to worry myself sick about you lopping off a finger or a hand."

Oh boy, he was sure in a bad mood. I wanted to know when the olds will buy me a pair of pull-on work boots like his and he said never. Apparently, the employer pays for the work tools and the regulation footwear out of a special employee's tool account. And they don't make steel-capped work boots in children's sizes, or for dwarfs.

I reminded Dad that type of labelling is defecating and the correct term is little people. He snorted and said I'd better look up defecating because he thought the word I meant was deprecating. (I did and he was right.)

By the time I left for Kirstie's, we had the first high bunk assembled. Both boys want to sleep in it. Finally Mum said they could top and tail. Dad said that set a precedent for the week as the other bunk won't be ready until next weekend at the earliest. There were bound to be tears before bedtime again and I was pleased to get out of there.

I noticed two things when I arrived for tea at the Jarretts. First, there was a baby crying. I didn't even know they had a baby! Second, something smelt good. My mother would learn to cook gourmet food too, if only my father was a hunter. But I was disappointed that we only had instant pudding and tinned fruit for afters.

Mrs Jarrett phoned my Dad to walk me home even though it's only half a block away. I could tell he was still grumpy because he told me not to shine that damned torch into the windows of the houses we went by.

To cheer him up, I used some of my poetic licence and told him the ice cream didn't melt in the oven because Mrs Jarrett had made the meringue perfectly. I said it was most spectacular Baked Alaska I've ever tasted. The only Baked Alaska. (Not.)

SUNDAY

Dad was right about that word. I'm glad I didn't use defecating in front of anyone else, though it might come in useful if we ever get a dog.

It's been raining all day and we stayed in the house and did nothing except sit, sit, sit. So I wrote a play. Thing One and Thing Two were played by Justin and Josh. They didn't have matching costumes, but that didn't matter. I was the Cat in The Hat.

Old Mrs Milton wandered over from next door with her cake tin under her umbrella. Aunt Julie, Uncle Pete and the cousins happened to drop by so it was a big audience for our small lounge. The twins got their parts mixed up and it was a bit of a flop, but I read somewhere that no playwright gets it right first time. Even Steven Spielberg wrote and performed neighbourhood plays first and it won't be long before I'll be working with professional actors in the future.

When they'd gone home I had to vacuum up the cake crumbs. Mum didn't care that I wanted to write down another story before it slipped out of my head. She said that's what notebooks are for. Half-way through I realised my storyline seemed familiar especially the dog that went around licking the kids in the gang.

Those Famous Five stories Mum used to read me had got into my head and I ended up throwing that story in the rubbish bin and starting again. I don't want to be sued.

I'm thinking of a pen name, though I don't want to be a George like that Orwell who wrote 1984 whose real name was Eric Blair. Though there's that woman writer who called herself George Eliot. She was Mary Anne Evans, but apparently it pays to have a man's name if you're a woman writer.

Aunt Helene says women are still disadvantaged. There's not many famous people named Ross so I might stay with that.

MONDAY

George Eliot is dead and has been for a long time and Kirstie was right after all. The start of the week is a Sunday and not Monday. I won't bring the subject up. As

I was walking home, I thought I saw Aunt Helene's blue Volkswagen Beetle go into the teacher's car park.

Josh was pulling me along as usual and for once I was glad to hurry as I wanted to go to the loo. So I didn't think about it too much as there's lots of cars around like hers.

Then Mum came home and told me Auntie would be here later, that she was at the school now talking to my teacher and they had something to discuss with me. I wanted to go to Kirstie's to talk about how my school records would need to be transferred to Kimble Primary, the closest school to Aunt Helene's in Kaiti. Then when Aunt Helene turned up I found I'm not leaving home.

Whew!

Instead I'm joining the Young Writers group! Auntie will be in charge of taking me to meetings. Also, I qualify for a five-day writer's camp for nine to fourteen-year olds next school holidays in Taupo. Auntie is applying for a scholarship to cover fees so I can attend. I didn't even know there were scholarships for things like that. I thought they were only for going to uni. Aunt Helene told me they need a few more nine and ten- year olds, because they have enough over-elevens.

Auntie says I have to be prepared to take it seriously, and do the writing exercises every day. That she's sticking her neck out for me and I'm a lucky girl. She's going to take me and stay for the camp so expects me to be on my best behaviour. She had a stack of papers in front of her. There's so much to take in and we mustn't talk about it publicly until the funding goes through.

Then I had to answer some personal questions like do you have night terrors and do you wet the bed?

"No," I said. "Not ever. I leave that for Justin because he's so good at it."

"Is that attitude necessary, Rosalyn?" said Mum. "You've made him cry. I'm not altogether convinced you're mature enough for such a unique opportunity."

Because I wanted to go so badly I kissed Justin and said sorry and although it was late by the time Aunt Helene left, I was allowed to go over and tell Kirstie before I hurried back for tea.

TUESDAY

The Māori land at Bastion Point has been on the news again. Dad reckons there should never have been a stand-off, they should have given it back to the original owners.

"It should never have been taken in the first place," said Mum, "for them to have to give it back."

"That's what I've been saying all the time, Esmé. You never listen properly."

This is the sort of pointless argument the olds have all the time. I wish I could go on a sit-in and hang out with protesters. I've never stayed on a marae. I'd take my sleeping bag and slippers and pay close attention to the kōrero. By the time the dispute was resolved I'd be speaking fluent Te Reo. I know I'd fit in because I like pork bones, spuds and watercress. At the school gala we always buy the hāngī.

Today Mr Morrissey was away. When we had to sit down and appreciate Victorian nonsense poetry Catherine Noland wanted to know what a five-pound note is and the relief teacher got Mr Morrissey's class pet Matt Branson to explain and he began, "On 10th July 1967 New Zealand changed from a pounds, shillings and pence currency we'd inherited since colonisation to decimal coinage..."

Matt can explain anything to do with finance. Aunt Helene says he has sold his soul to mammon. I must ask her what that means. I winked at Kirstie and tilted my head to indicate where she should be looking. Across the room while the relief teacher was writing on the board Noel Perkins had his hand down his pants again. He's been told he must keep both hands on his desk.

Matt Branson was droning on and on. The imperial system was British-based and cumbersome, Mr Muldoon, who was Finance Minister then went on to become Prime Minister, but his true success was ...

If boring was an Olympic sport we would pick up a gold medal every time with Matt.

I saw Ben Marks about to flick a paper dart at Melissa O'Brien. She wouldn't have seen it coming as she had laid her head down on her arms and fallen asleep.

Charlie Davis went oink-oink-oink as we reached the bit where the piggy-wig stood in the wood. He was the only one getting into the spirit of the nonsense poem. Mr Morrissey would never have put up with all this but the relief teacher cleared his throat.

"Thank you, Matthew," he said. "Sit down, please. A five-pound note is like a ten-dollar bill, Catherine. However, the most commonly asked question about The Owl and the Pussycat concerns the runcible spoon."

He paused.

"Are you paying attention, Samuel Shaw?"

Obviously, Sam wasn't. He was drawing cartoons and yawning. Dad reads poetry the best, but he doesn't like us telling anyone in case they think he's a poetry nerd.

WEDNESDAY

What did Aunt Helene say to Mr Morrissey? He's been looking at me all day as if I came from a different planet.

The Bible in Schools lady told us a story about birthright. I said that even if Jacob and Esau did look alike, unless they find the bodies they can never prove if they were identical or fraternal twins. I should know. Our own twins look like each other, but we can't afford to get them tested.

She said, "Thank you, Rosalie Johnson." (She can never get anyone's name right.) "Why don't you come up front and teach the class?"

When I did, she got mad. How was I to know she was being sarcastic?

Today the Perfect Six brought their Cabbage Patch Kids into class. You don't buy them, you adopt them, they told us. Anyway, although they're not in the shops, you can order a Cabbage Patch Kid from somewhere, overseas, I think, if you're willing to pay mega-bucks and Victoria just had to have one of her very own, She's so spoilt. Then so did her other five gang members.

Of course!

They didn't like it when Mr Morrissey told them to put them away in their schoolbags. I saw Elizabeth Lewis's lower lip tremble for a moment. She nearly cried. Valerie Dixon, the nicest member of the Perfect Six gang, lives opposite the school gates. She asked if she could take her little Mandy Beth home and put her to bed.

"They're not dolls," Alison Morris told him, "they're our babies."

Mr Morrissey said he had no objection to them playing with their offspring during breaks, but they must stay in their bags during class time.

Kirstie went over to the Perfect Six during morning break and said she'd bring her toy monkey Curious George in tomorrow. Victoria Allen only shrugged and turned away, saying whatever as if she didn't care, but I noticed she wasn't smiling as she usually does when she thinks she's got the better of you.

Jennifer Sorren was standing close by and claimed to have a real living doll and promised to bring it over tomorrow after school. She wanted Kirstie and as many of the girls as possible, especially the Perfect Six, to come over to my place and see for themselves.

By now I was bored with all this talk of dolls as they've never been my thing. I figured Jennifer's would be something ordinary, nothing as expensive as a Cabbage Patch Kid.

After lunch Victoria pretended her doll was crying out in the corridor and something in her bag was definitely making a noise. Maybe some other noisy wind-up toy she'd forgotten about that had turned itself on. That was real freaky, like that Minnie Dean infant murderer who put a baby in a hat box.

I told Kirstie all about the Winton baby farmer, the only woman in New Zealand to be hung. My aunt says poor Minnie was falsely accused of killing babies and should never have got the death sentence. Babies often died way back in the 1890s because mothers used laudanum to help them sleep and it was like poison.

Aunt Helene should know. I've seen the book she's got about Minnie Dean by an author called Hudd or something like that.

Victoria's model must have been more advanced than the other five dolls if it really could cry though. She went mental when Mr Morrissey wouldn't allow her to check on her baby. I think I'm in bad with her, too.

I had this awful feeling that Victoria might have overheard me call her *precious baby* a model because she gave me a real dirty look. By then all the *mothers* were in tears because Victoria was so upset and it started some of the other girls bawling too.

Valerie Dixon boo-hooed to Mr Morrissey about it being a long day for tired, overheated baby Mandy Beth zipped up in a bag. I must admit her description did sound like child abuse. Victoria wouldn't shut up. What a drama.

Oh please! They're only dolls. It had stopped being amusing long before our teacher totally lost control of the class. I looked across and saw him squeezing his head between his hands and grinding his teeth.

Then everyone started talking and Charlie, Ben and a couple of the boys began running around the room. I was about to go to the office to get help when Mr Collinson came in. He must have heard the noise because he often walks around the classrooms.

After hearing the story Mr Collinson suggested *all* the dolls be taken across the road to Valerie Dixon's place. We watched Mr Collinson pass through the shared corridor into the senior classroom.

Shortly after we looked through the windows to watch Mrs Girton leading the Perfect Six out of the school grounds cuddling their six stupid babies.

Good riddance. Peace at last.

Mr Collinson won't have liked that because he was left teaching Mrs Girton's class for ages and ages. But I guess it takes a long time to put a baby down for a nap and dry everyone's tears. Knowing elephant-legs Girton she probably had her feet up sipping a cup of tea with Valerie's Bible-basher mother while she waited.

It's good that things came to crisis point because I bet notes will be sent home tonight and the Perfect Six will be told to *never* bring the Cabbage Patch Kids to school ever again. Serves them right. Ha ha.

THURSDAY

I can't believe what happened. When we got home after school, I settled the twins with peanut butter sammies, kicked off my skirt and had changed into my orange jeans when Jennifer Sorren walked up our drive pushing a real pram.

I'd forgotten about her promise to bring a doll over and I was about to say that pram's a bit much for something you bought from a toyshop when it started to shake and wail and when I peeked inside there was a human baby in there.

I sort of forgot Jennifer had a baby sister. I wish the Perfect Six had been around to see her, but none of them have ever been to my house.

FRIDAY

We were doing Early New Zealand history when a messenger came for me. Mr Morrissey whispered in my ear that I was needed in the infants' classroom to change Justin's pants. Miss Downes, his teacher, said normally he would've been sent home, but they couldn't do that where there was a working mother and how lucky Justin was to have a big sister in the same school.

Yeah, right! Lucky for *him*! I didn't even know he had a packet of baby wet wipes with his spare pair of shorts and underpants. I'd sort of forgotten Mum said Justin might have an accident. Like a wet messy fart sort of accident. His pants were soaking.

I should be used to that by now, but I nearly threw up when I changed his skid-marked underpants. I used his wet shorts to sort of clean him up a bit then shoved everything back in the same plastic bag his clean ones had been in.

I didn't wipe his bottom properly. Too gross! Didn't even open the wet wipes packet. Besides, where would I put those used wet wipes? Mr Collinson keeps telling us we're not allowed to flush foreign objects down the loo's.

He reminds us (but not the boys for some reason) not to flush things down the toilets. When they have to get the plumber in for blocked toilets the teachers always blame the girls. Why? I just don't get it.

Back in class it was obvious they all wanted to know where I'd been.

"Are you in trouble?" asked Victoria Allen.

"Oh, no," I said. "I was called to the Principal's office because it seems I'm in for some prize, but I'm not allowed to talk about it yet."

Her jaw dropped in disbelief. It's not exactly a lie. Mr Morrissey didn't say anything, thank goodness, probably because Nancy and Lori get called to infants for the same thing now and then. I expect Kirstie will find out all about it next year when ginormous Jimmy starts school.

When she got home, Mum asked if I could please remember to put Justin's wet and dirty pants in the bucket to soak.

"Maybe Justin should go back to kindergarten," I said.

Mum frowned. "Justin is a sensitive child. He'd hate that." (And as kindy is only half-days, she'd have to quit work.)

Apparently, I need to be more patient with Justin because Josh and I are more emotionally robust. (Must look that up.) Then she fished out a note from Miss Downes and read it to me, frowning again.

"Please ask Rosalyn to freshen her brother up using the wet wipes you've provided. This will save him from developing a rash and keep him smelling fresh."

Who do they think I am? That famous early New Zealand Nurse Maude we read about last week? Or the confounded Elgin district nurse who visits once a term?

SATURDAY

I decided to make a stand on that stupid name the olds gave me. I told them at breakfast I will only answer to Roz or Ross. Anyway, we were back from Mum's work, and I was swinging in the hammock in my white hipster jeans and purple waistcoat when Mum called us by name. I knew she had some job lined up for *Rosalyn* so I totally ignored her. That'd teach her!

She called again. "Rosalyn, this is your last warning. If you don't answer, you're going to regret it."

Two minutes later the twins ran past with a chocolate bar each. We hardly ever get chocolate! My parents must have grown up in the depression with rationing. Then she calmly sat down with a cup of tea and ate my bar one square at a time. I nearly whacked Josh for standing right in front of me saying yum yum between bites.

"Well, Rosalyn," said Dad, "I guess your Mum has called your bluff."

Whatever!

I always knew they loved the twins more than me. The two of them were so mean I ended up going over to Lori's.

I might go and live with Aunt Helene after all.

SUNDAY

So the week starts here, on a Sunday. Technically. I did point out to Kirstie that the Bible in School teachers wouldn't agree with her. Christians say it's Monday because God rested on the seventh day and so should we.

You know, I'm so over babies and I don't just mean Cabbage Patch babies. Mrs Next-Door (I call her that because her name's too difficult to say or spell) came over carrying her latest baby. She was bawling so loudly Mum put the jug on and shooed us outside.

Yes, even Dad. He mumbled, "Women's troubles. Wouldn't stay if you paid me," and went into the shed to finish building the other high bunk bed.

Over the noise of Dad's table-saw I managed to hear some of it, though Mrs Next Door's accent is hard to understand. She and her husband come from somewhere starting with A – could be Albania or Argentina or Arkansas.

She said something about an examination being painful. She's right about that. When we have exams at school, especially maths, they're always painful.

Then she was wailing about her husband and too many babies – she does have a lot – and about the priest and her mother-in-law, and that she couldn't do it. I expect she's been too busy with those babies to sit down and study. Mum told her she should do it.

"Think of the children you already have. Who will care for them if they lose their mother?"

At that I stood by the kitchen door and started waving so Mum would see me. I was mouthing NO! Mrs Next-Door was standing with her back to me, the baby over her shoulder, puking. It's always puking. I didn't want Mum taking on any more kids. Mum put her hands on her hips and glared at me.

"Did you want something, Rosalyn?"

There's no point talking to her when she's in one of her moods, so I backed down.

"Some juice and a sandwich, please, Mum."

When I got them, I asked if I could go and play with Kirstie. Not that playing was on my mind. I won't be able to cope if we end up with two or three of Mrs Next-Door's babies.

Mum told me I could go and shut the back door while I was still on the doorstep. When I come back I'll explain how dramatised I've been having to change Justin's wet skid-marked underpants.

Kirstie and I went to our secret hide-out beside the railway line. For once she listened without interrupting then said, "Perhaps the word you mean is traumatised."

"No," I said. "I do mean dramatised, because there's too much going on around me and it's stressing me out."

I didn't want to admit I had it wrong. I came back too late to help with bunk building and Dad's finished it anyway. The boys' room smells of new timber, which is an improvement on the usual smells. Pissing and wet farting!

The twins were happy and went early to bed and Mum sent Dad up to read them a story. Sometimes Justin and Josh are OK, but I still don't want Mum adding to the family. Especially after what happened with the Sorren baby when Jennifer brought it over on Thursday. It's a nice enough baby, as babies go, and Jennifer and I were going to take it to Kirstie's because their baby is a girl, too, and the two of them might become best friends.

We had to wait until Mum got home and the first thing she asked was if Jennifer's mother knew exactly where her baby was. Jennifer stared at her feet and said, "Sort of, but it's all right. My mother won't mind."

Then Mum rang Mrs Sorren and she was crying so loud we could hear her even though Mum was out in the hall. When she woke from her afternoon nap and found her baby gone and no note she thought Julia had been stolen and the police were already on their way.

They ended up coming to our house instead and the neighbours stood in the street to watch Jennifer, baby and pram loaded into the police car.

I wish they had put on the siren, though.

MONDAY

I walked straight past Miss Downes today after taking the boys to their classroom. I had my hand cupped over my mouth so she'd never know I was poking my tongue out. She smiled sweetly and said, "So glad your mother mentioned my note on proper hygiene, Rosalyn."
I invited Jennifer Sorren over after school, but she reckons she's banned from going anywhere until she's twelve at least. Serves her right, I suppose. She should have thought to leave a note. She's so tragically sad about it I won't be surprised if she runs away and we end up looking for her body in the swamp like you see on the news.

TUESDAY

My first meeting at Gisborne Young Writers is on Thursday from 4 until 6.30pm. I'm so excited! I'm going to wear my pink shirt and my indigo jeans. Writers must dress for their public!

I expect I will have to get used to coming home to a cold dinner and the jealousy of the Perfect Six. They say great artists and writers must suffer for their art.

As time goes by I will need to make an effort not to become a stranger to my little brothers, knowing how hard it must be them to have such a talented big sister. Perhaps if they're lucky they can find something they're good at, too. Can't think what.

WEDNESDAY

One more day. I've got two notebooks like reporters use and four black biros. Aunt Helene says it's common to use blue biro and it doesn't photocopy well if you want to make extra copies.

THURSDAY

Today's the day. I'll probably be the only child from a working-class background at the Young Writers group. I expect they all go to private schools, and own their own ponies. I won't let on that I live in squalor.
More later!!

Whew. Didn't get back until twenty past seven. Mum had chicken casserole and mashed potato keeping hot in the oven. I was expecting to go to bed on a peanut butter sammie and a glass of milk.

Justin must have missed me as he crawled up on my knee as I ate. Mum and Dad were eager to hear all about it and I did my best, but it's tiring on the brain stretching what Mr Reilly called our creative muscles. I told the olds I'd read them one of my writing exercises tomorrow.

Mr Reilly said to call him Seamus and that he's not our teacher, he's our facilitator. He's brilliant! He's a lot younger than Mr Morrissey and he's been published! He read us a poem from his first collection, Conversations with the Past.

He told us it's dedicated it to his wife Noelene. She's coming on the course with him. I had a quick shower and went straight to bed.

FRIDAY

Mr Morrissey made me put away my exercise book that I've labelled GREAT IDEAS. That wasn't a good start to the morning. Should he even be teaching if he can't be fully engaged in extending a future writer and journalist like me?

I tried to explain we writers were supposed to keep a notebook by us at all times and jot down notes when the muse visited. That Mr Reilly said our ideas book was the key to unlock our treasure trove of latent stories. Mr Morrissey spoke gruffly. Put it away, Rosalyn. I can't make an exception for one pupil, can I? (Yes, he could.)

Ben Marks was watching us and I guess he had been drawing cartoons on his pad and Charlie Davis had his desk up, about to take out his colouring book again. At break Kirstie asked me if she was still my best friend.

She said she thought I'd be off doing equestrian things with my writing group pals this weekend. I didn't tell her none of them owns a horse.

SATURDAY

It's awesome how I am beginning to see people as characters now that I can put in a book or interview. The twins were busy feeding the ducks while we waited for Mum and I decided to ask the old wino who sleeps under the bridge if he'd like to share his story with me.

He was there in his usual spot, wrapped in a dozen smelly old coats. I'd barely taken one step towards him when Mum turned up and shouted at me.

"Rosalyn, what's got into you lately? Come here this instant. This instant. Now!"

Her face was bright red and she was yelling, "You're supposed to be watching the boys."

She must be having a nervous breakdown because I WAS watching them. They were only a few yards away. Dad wasn't happy when Mum complained to him about it, either. He gave me *both* his favourite lectures on stranger danger and the importance of supervising kids near water. Then he sent me to my room to think about what I'd done wrong.

The olds have got no idea what it takes to be a journalist. You've got to be prepared to step out of your comfort zone, to discover slice of life stories and make them live on the page!

While I was imprisoned in my room I started working on a story about Rhamat of Bangladesh.

Seamus told us to hook the reader with our opening statement, so here goes. In the slums of Bangladesh lives nine-year old Rhamat. Six days a week he works in a factory from dawn to dusk sewing buttons on shirts for a US clothing company.

A half-hour lunch break is all the child workers get, a cup of cold rice and ten rupees is what they earn.
(I'd better check that. Facts are important to support your story, says Seamus.)

I could turn this into a picture book for little children. Naturally, I'll have to find a professional illustrator for the front cover. Or I could do my own drawings. I'm a lot better than I was last year. That how to draw book I got from Gran for my birthday improved my drawing out of sight. Black on white to save on costs, though I've got some ideas for fundraising.

My writing tutor says it's expensive to publish so I'll probably only order five thousand copies for the first print run. Matt Branson can help me with the sums. It'll be good practice if he's going to be my accountant later on. All the profits from that first five thousand can go to World Vision. That will attract good publicity.

One day I hope to be rich enough to bring Rhamat to

live in New Zealand. That'll make a good documentary. It will be good if he can speak some English. I hope Victoria Allen will be watching.

I expect I will be ten years old or maybe eleven before I can fly to Bangladesh. Aunt Helene can be my travel companion since she's been the only one to believe in me and nurture my talents.

Her and Madame Bovary. I've read travellers need to take their own drinking water because the food and water in India and Bangladesh is too polluted.

Anyway, the film crew will sort all that out and before I write any more of Rhamat I'll get a book out of the library on Indian children in the workforce. Especially the kids who live in slums.

SUNDAY

Went to our grandmother's today for our Sunday outing. She laughed and said, "Your generation would have never survived the Depression. You go without a bit of chocolate and you think you're hard done by,"

Then she went on to tell me Mum was her youngest child and spoilt. I know Mum is a couple of years younger than Dad. Every time I ask her how old she is, she always says, I'm the same age as my tongue, and a little older than my teeth. Gran says it's rude to ask a lady her age.

Why? When Gran lived in the old villa on the quarter acre with all the big trees I always wanted to stay overnight, but now she's in one of those white brick old people's flats with no back yard. I hate it because it's hard to keep the boys from running around.

We haven't been back since Josh broke the china cat that stood by her door. I was on the back porch with the twins, who were looking really grown up in the long trousers Gran had sewn for them. This time Josh was wearing the darker pair, which they both prefer.

The olds were talking.

"I've got an appointment next week with the doctor," Mum said. "The pill is making me sick."

"Oh, dear, Esmé. What will you do?"

"That's what I'm going to ask the doctor about."

I didn't want to let on I was listening, but if it's only one little pill that's making her sick, surely there's no need to take time off work to go and see the doctor? Mum's a real drama queen. Gran shouted us lunch at the R.S.A. She gets senior rates there. They don't have gourmet food on the menu. Gran says you don't need to wear your best bib and tucker and that's true because the old man at the next table had his tucker all down the front of him. Tucker is another word for food and it would've been a good idea to keep a few grown-up towelling bibs behind the counter.

The adults ordered the special of the day, mince on toast. I refused the children's menu and amazed the staff with my knowledge of cooking seafood. I could tell Gran was impressed too from the way she kept staring at me.

I asked intelligent questions on every dish until the waiter got a bit grumpy. In the end I settled for mince on toast, too, but mine had a side order of Greek salad with yoghurt dressing.

Justin and Josh had chicken drumsticks with chips, served with a pathetic helping of tomato sauce. Josh opened his mouth to complain and Justin told him to stuff it.

For once I was almost proud of them for their good table manners though they still eat with their mouths open. When Dad mentioned I was the youngest member of the local junior writers group, Gran poked me in the ribs.

"Now don't you go developing an exaggerated sense of

your own self-importance, my child," she said.

As if!

MONDAY

What is it with our place? Lately girls and women always seem to be coming over and crying. Isobel Sorren is crying because her little sister has gone missing.

No, not baby Julia this time. Its Jennifer. Seeing it was an emergency, I left Mum a note to say the twins were next door. Mrs Milton called me the salt of the earth and was only too pleased to help, considering I was on a search and rescue mission concerning life and death. Isobel and I hurried straight over to the swamp-lands, stopping to pick up Kirstie along the way.

I didn't want to upset Isobel more by letting on I was looking for a body when I was pushing a long stick into the water.

Once, in the swamps, my stick did hit something solid that was nothing but a water-logged tree branch. When it started to get dark we decided to go home. Oh no! Not again! The police car was parked at my house.

Talk about day sha voo! The police must be getting sick and tired of the Sorrens losing their daughters. Next thing, Mrs Sorren will start losing her two sons.

Mum was making the police officer and Mrs Sorren a cup of tea when I walked up our driveway with Isobel and Kirstie. Why do grown-ups think a cup of tea will solve any problem? They'd found Jennifer hours ago feeding chickens. She was hiding at Mrs Maxwell's in the next street, the President of the Poultry Fanciers Club.

When will Jennifer learn to leave a note? Isobel is much more sensible than Jennifer. Mrs Sorren read out Isobel's note. It said, 3.28pm. Gone to Jondells. I know Roz will lead us straight to Jennifer. Dead or alive we won't rest until we find her. Isobel. PS Don't let Warner and Vinny eat my tea.

Madame Bovary was worth those two fifty cents. I hope the police officer noticed how highly Isobel believes in my intuition. They might use me next time they're hunting for missing people.

Kirstie's Mum had rung mine several times because it was getting so dark and late and she had to go straight home. The parents have all ganged up together and agreed on a group punishment.

Now none of us is allowed to go anywhere after school for a week. Kirstie, me and Isobel and Jennifer, of course, who before she ran away, was already in trouble for taking the baby. Kirstie got another hiding with her father's belt. Not fair. We were only trying to help.

TUESDAY

Boring as. Nothing to look forward to after school. Kirstie showed me the marks on her back.

WEDNESDAY

Outside of school, I'm becoming a hermit. Too scared to ask if I'm allowed to go to writers' group tomorrow. Kirstie thinks the marks from her father's belt might be infected.

THURSDAY

Mum said she was in two minds about letting me go to Young Writers tonight. Two minds? I didn't want to say anything, but she should be more careful about saying stuff like that. It sounds psycho to me. What if a doctor heard her? She might be sent to a mental hospital.

"Helene's invested time and money in the child, Esmé," said Dad. "We can't let that go to waste."

Mum sniffed. "Yes, but on the other hand, if we're seen to back down, well, it's the principle of the thing, isn't it?"

In the end, I was allowed to go. When she dropped me home, Aunt Helene stayed to join me for a late tea. The subject of missing children is banned from the dinner table.

The twins were crawling round and round the table in their dressing gowns, each pushing a toy car. They were playing police officers.

FRIDAY

Jennifer, Isobel, Kirstie and me are hanging around together. The other kids have no understanding of the trauma we've been through.

Isobel says Kirstie should get her bruises seen to, but Kirstie is worried if the visiting school district nurse is informed, she might be put in a home or foster care.

Jennifer says we should listen to Isobel because she's ten and has more life experience, being so much older. In the end, we all agreed. If Kirstie's back hasn't healed by Monday, we will tell.

SATURDAY

Day five of my isolation. Today when we were feeding the ducks, I saw the homeless man under the bridge. I waved, but kept my distance. It's sad no one gives a toss about him. I'm disgusted by how uncaring our city is. I'm going to interview him when I'm all grown up. I told Mum so.

"Rosalyn," she said, you're talking almost ten years from now. It's common knowledge Desmond Burton is a chronic alcoholic with irreversible liver damage."

"Why doesn't someone take him to AA then?"

She sighed. "Because he won't go. He's too sick and he's in denial. Most alcoholics are. He's taken to A & E at least once a month, usually when he's found unconscious. Believe me, he's been offered every form of help, including decent housing, but … oh, well, it's one of those things."

I'm still going to interview him. The moment I'm eighteen and legally an adult. Mum can't stop me. I told her so. When I got home after returning from Mum's work I went straight to my room and stayed there to get away from her negativity. And Dad's as bad!

I refused to mow the lawn. Dad can do it himself. Hahahaha. I don't care if they dock my pocket money. Besides, I'm still on punishment and can't go out anyway. I sat down at my desk and wrote up a heading.

Desmond Burton
A sick old man thoughtlessly cast aside
by an uncaring community.
By Roz Jondell.

When I was nine, I'd wait with my twin brothers for our Mum to finish her Saturday shift at the Americano, the local fast food diner.

There, on the riverbank, near the Old Colonial Bridge was when I first noticed an old man huddled under its steel girders, his only possessions a bottle in a paper bag and a pile of old coats.

I was forbidden by my mother to talk to him, and my father punished me when I tried to walk towards him. I couldn't believe how mean both parents were to me over this incident. Now that I'm eighteen, and legally an adult, I take up where I left off...

Not bad, but it could be better before it goes into his folder. Nine years is a long way off, so there's plenty of time to get it right. I'm still not sure if I'll be Roz or Ross by then. I guess I could use both. I'll never write as Rosalyn.

Could be I won't even be Jondell by then. I'd better work on getting my pen name right for when I'm published and famous. What's already been written about Desmond Burton in the local papers?

Next time I go to the library I'll ask how I can check that out. Wish I could go to the Sorren's or Kirstie's. My Dad sent Macey Liddicott home. She lives four blocks away.

I tapped on my bedroom window, but she couldn't hear me. I didn't dare bang too hard and break the glass. I'm in enough trouble. I should have made a sign to hold up. Help. I'm a prisoner. Too late now.

Macey has walked away. I'm like Rapunzel without the long hair, watching the world go by. Dad had to turn off the mower to talk to Macey. Now he's having trouble starting it again. Ha ha. Serves him right.

SUNDAY

I'm the only one whose curfew didn't finish last night, so still no visitors all day. I had another day added because of going to Young Writers on Thursday night. The boys sound like American kids, thanks to Sesame Street. They want tuna-fish with mayonnaise for lunch.

Tuna-fish! What's that? We don't say, I'll have a beef-meat sandwich, do we?

Mum opened up a tin of sardines, tipped them on their plates and smothered them with her homemade salad dressing made from Highlander condensed milk. She announced, "This is the Kiwi equivalent of tuna-fish and mayonnaise. Eat it up."

They ate it up.

MONDAY

Kirstie isn't going into foster care after all. Her back's all better. Curfew is over, and after school we're going back to her place. Now I know what it's like going to prison, and it's true what they say.

You don't appreciate freedom until you lose it. Mum's yelling down the hall, Get your lazy butt off to school, young lady. She keeps moaning she'd like a different job. She'd make a good prison warder.

TUESDAY

Too busy catching up on freedom to write much. Oh, and homework. Why can't teachers teach us what we need to know while we're at school? They're paid enough to do their job properly.

WEDNESDAY

Still getting used to being out of prison and Mum made me clean my cell. And I wanted to finish reading Heidi. It's about this girl being sent away like what nearly happened to me.

Now I know all about alpine huts with a sleeping loft. They have to have steeped pitched roofs for the snow to slide off. I think I will have a go at building one like the illustrations in this book someday. Especially if I go to live in Otira in Arthur's Pass.

Mr Reilly says all good writers also read a lot and he's right. You learn heaps from books and get some really good ideas too.

THURSDAY

We're trying out a new system for Thursday night. Aunt Helene took me to Young Writers and I stayed overnight in her spare room.

I like sitting up in the double bed to write in my diary and she's got a painting on the wall I like to look at, though I can't work out exactly what it's about.

When I asked Aunt Helene she shrugged and said it was enigmatic.

She bought it in France when she spent a year in Europe. It takes a little time to get to sleep here as every time I move, the waterproof mattress cover rustles. Eventually she'll figure out I don't need it.

I've been having a sneak read of her feminist books. Someone called Shulamith Firestone thinks in future babies will be hatched in incubators. Maybe that's why Aunt Helene has never got married. She doesn't want babies the old-fashioned way.

Tonight my aunt's best friend Sarah came over. They must have had a quarrel because Sarah arrived with flowers and wine and I heard her whisper, "Forgive me, Helene." She brought salmon and asparagus for tea and Aunt Helene served it up with a yummy cheese sauce, baked yams and sliced beetroot simmered in orange juice and ginger.

Thanks to her influence my appreciation of fine cuisine is developing. Sarah decided not to drive home because she'd been drinking wine and because I'm in the spare room they had to top and tail in Aunt Helene's bedroom. They've gone to bed now and she must still be a bit cross with Sarah because I heard them arguing again and they didn't stop until my aunt said, Not tonight. Not with my niece in the house. She's good like that about things. Like not letting her friend play loud music because I need my sleep.

FRIDAY

Aunt Helene dropped me home this morning by seven in time to change and get ready for school. The skirt I wanted to wear wasn't on my bedroom floor and I had to get it out of the washing basket in the laundry.

If I didn't have to walk my little brothers to school, Aunt Helene could drop me straight at the school gate. It's not fair. She said she does know what it's like to do things you don't want to and we all have to get used to it and I'd better toughen up.

Going to Young Writers is my time off from the twins and walking them to school is our time together. When she was my age she took my Dad to school and changed his pants.

At school Mr Morrissey went on and on about the importance of maths as a life skill. He looked straight at Victoria and Catherine when he said you need maths to measure ingredients for baking and then at Matt and Sam when he added and to get the numbers right if you're building a deck.

That's like what Dad keeps saying, "Timber needs to be measured accurately."

I told him we're being raised to have what Aunt Helene calls fluid gender roles at our house. Dad's always moaning that the majority of single women he does plumbing work for live in houses that need lots of structural maintenance and it's because women rely on men to do it for them.

He wants all his kids to have basic D.I.Y No. 8 skills. I said I already use most of Dad's tools and I mow the lawns. Josh is learning to cook omelettes and Justin folds the washing, thank goodness. Before that, I had to do everything.

That led into a classroom discussion on pocket money and chores. Charlie Davis says his job is to walk his father home every Friday and Saturday. Charlie likes it when the other drunks at the pub give him their spare change.

Melissa O'Brien doesn't get pocket money and has to

take the little kids into her Nana's room before she comes to school. Her mother can't get out of bed till noon.

At morning break Kirstie told me I sound like a women's libber. What's wrong with that, I said, and who can blame me? You haven't got an aunt like mine.

While I was stacking dishes after tea I overheard Dad say to Mum, "So Rosalyn mentioned Sarah swung by Helene's for tea last night."

I hadn't told him she stayed the night. He went on, "Looks like she's back on the scene. Rather her than that awful Rhonda. Never had time for her. Too harsh and radical."

"The name's Wanda, not Rhonda," said Mum, "and she's moved to Napier apparently and good riddance I say. When they've settled down a bit, we'll have Helene and Sarah around for tea."

"If that's what you want," said Dad. "Now let me read my paper in peace."

SATURDAY

Still thinking about my short-term writing goals, my medium-term writing goals and my long-term writing goals. It's taking me some time to figure them out, but I will get around to it.

SUNDAY

Kirstie came over after lunch. She brought her diary and we made a secret pact with a needle. Pricked our fingers and spat on them. Then we put spots of mixed blood and spit on the front and back of each diary. We ended up sitting on pillows hard up against my bedroom door because we couldn't lock it. Then we swapped diaries.

Her secrets are safe with me. Kirstie is mad she has to change their baby's nappies though they're not Karitane yellow anymore. Jimmy still has accidents sometimes and it's not only wet pants. Yuk. And I thought Justin's bed-wetting was bad, but there's nothing Kirstie doesn't know about the downside of babies and she definitely has it worse.

We've sworn a blood oath. No children for us. Ever. When her Dad comes back from being away in the bush her mother is lazy and won't do any housework the next day because they mostly stay in the bedroom with the door shut. He must get worn out carrying all those possum traps about. No wonder he needs his sleep.

Today I learned that day shar voo is spelt déjà vu and it's bandeau not bando. No wonder I couldn't find it in my dictionary. How was I to know it's French? I could have asked Françoise in the senior class. She was born in France.

I told Kirstie that Aunt Helene wasn't my age at all like she told me when my father started school. She was twelve. She took my Dad into the infant room every morning before biking off to Central Intermediate. Kirstie says both my Mum and Dad sound like change of life babies.

If Auntie is thirty-nine then that makes my Dad thirty-two. Then Mum must be thirty. Nothing wrong with my basic maths, thank you, Mr Morrissey. Put that in your next report.

Poor Aunt Helene. It must be awful to be nearly forty. I try hard to be patient with old people, but it's not easy. Kirsty says that her Dad's forty already.

That explains why he gets annoyed so easily. Kirstie doesn't know her mother's age yet. Kirstie and I are going to have a reading diary day together after I get back from camp in the school holidays.

MONDAY

Mr Morrissey reminded us the school term breaks up on Friday. Like we need reminding! We take our reports home mid-week. They need to be returned and signed by Friday morning.

Melissa O'Brien says they don't have a pen in their house. Mr Morrissey is lending her one.

TUESDAY

Roll on Friday.

WEDNESDAY

My mother read my report first and all she said was, "That's nice, dear." What does that even mean? I wanted to jot down everything Mr Morrissey wrote but the olds said the report was addressed to them.

I was allowed to read it, but they gave me no time to copy it. Under maths, Mr Morrissey wrote, Rosalyn has obvious ability but doesn't apply herself. Could do better.

Dad sounds just like him when he talks about maths being part of everyday life. I reminded him I only need to be a mediocre mathematician when I grow up. When I'm rich and famous, I'll have an accountant, probably Matt Branson, to manage my finances – staff wages, investments, things like that.

Dad sighed and said, "If not when, Rosalyn," then he signed my report, and sealed the envelope.

THURSDAY

Mr Morrissey was already sitting at his desk when we walked into the classroom. We had to line up and hand him our reports before taking our seats.

Melissa O'Brien was crying. She told him the dog ate his pen. He raised his eyebrows, but said nothing and held out his hand for the signed report. She cried harder and said her Mum used it to light the fire because they had no newspaper left.

He told her he'd find another copy and when he gave it to her after lunch, there was a stack of old newspapers with it. I wasn't able to stay at Kirstie's long after school. Young Writers wasn't on tonight, but I had to go home to pack for camp.

FRIDAY

The holidays begin at three today. Yippee! No school for two weeks. No taking little brothers into town tomorrow. Mum is home for the next fortnight.

Besides, Aunt Helene arrives after school to pick me up. I'm sitting on my bag in the driveway writing this. We'll be at Morere Hot Springs tonight and arrive at Nana's in Napier on Saturday.

I must have slept in the car because next thing I knew we were there and Aunt Helene was unloading the car. We have a cabin with two sets of bunk beds to ourselves. There was barely enough time for a hot dip in the main complex before closing time and the other pools are a fifteen-minute walk through the bush.

Just as well she brought some food to cook because there's no shops in Morere. Just a hot pool and the camping ground is way out in the bush on the road between Gisborne and Wairoa.

I thought I'd outgrown baked beans and a tin of tomatoes cooked together on toast but it was delicious. Perhaps only because I was so tired and hungry. We had salami in the chiller box too, but I left that for Aunt Helene, it's a bit too spicy for me.

SATURDAY

Aunt Helene woke me early and we were the first through the gate when the pools opened. She was keen to tramp to the top pools. I said she could go by herself and I'd jump into the main pool.

She pointed to the sign that read no unsupervised children and made me puff my way uphill to the bush track pools. I wish I'd bought more than one swimsuit like Mum suggested. Instead, I stayed in the dressing shed wrapped in my towel. Aunt Helene dipped my wet swimwear into the pool and handed it to me all steaming.

Still, it was hard to pull on. I was the only child there. You can only sit in these pools. They're hotter and there's no room for swimming around. Grown-ups prefer them. I can tell from the amount of old people sitting about. Boring. I'd rather swim down the track at the main pool.

For brunch we had a can of bully-beef on Vogel's toast, with tinned tomatoes and baked beans again. No wonder I'm so weak. That tramp to the bush pool, and the bully-beef was the first meat protein I've had since leaving Gisborne yesterday.

I have no intention of becoming a vegetarian. There was one other family using the cookhouse and an old couple with a camper van. We took turns with the tin opener and there should have been more than one wooden spoon. I wrote that in the visitor book under suggestions for improvement. Tins flowed out of the rubbish bin. I'm so over canned food.

Now it's 3.17pm in Napier and we're at Nana's and it's turning into a proper holiday. No taking twins on the bus today. I was sent up for an afternoon nap in the spare room with all Nana's homemade stuffed dolls and bears.

The door was half-open and I heard Aunt Helene say,

"For heaven's sake. I'm 39 years old. You'd think I'd be entitled to some information after all this time. Thirty-nine."

That figures. I already worked out that she was twelve when my Dad was five. Nana was saying, "It was the best thing to do, Helen, under the circumstances. He was still in high school himself, far too young to marry and support you. Then there was your reputation to consider. As your mother I had to ..."

That's when my aunt used words I've never even heard her mutter.

"Do you think I give a flying F about any of that S? We all know marriage is a patriarchal institution." (Hope I spelt that right.)

"Keep your voice down, dear," said Nana, and after that I only heard parts of the conversation. "You haven't found the right man yet and how many times must I tell you that Sarah and I ..."

By now my ears were buzzing from flapping so hard and I was glad when Nana said, "Let's talk about something else, please." I was glad because now I'd hear what they thought about me. There was something about Steve and Nana said Esmé was the making of that lad, and even the sweet wee twins, bless them. I must have missed the part about me.

In the end, I got back onto the bed and finished my writing requirements for camp, including my list of short, medium and long-term writing goals.

That night Aunt Helene got to share that room with a hundred and one stuffed toys and dolls and I thought I'd get a mattress on the floor, which always reminds me of camping. But Nana made me sleep on some saggy old canvas camp bed in the lounge next to the cane shelving full of dolls of the world.

I couldn't turn over and I woke up with a sore back. Now I know what it was like for Papa in the trenches.

SUNDAY

More of the same at Nana's. I'm back in the spare room writing notes. They said I could stay in the lounge with them, but it was too boring. I didn't realise there were so many people with hernias and varicose veins and something piles that means you can't sit down. And the others waiting for operations for knees and hips.

I don't ever want to be over fifty. I did hear my name mentioned once, but only briefly. That was before they started talking about my great-aunt Constance's operation for something that had prolapsed, whatever that means. I couldn't stop yawning.

Near tea time, I was horrified to see Nana cooking in those old heavy aluminium three-cornered pots. You take them off the stove with a lever. She sees nothing wrong with putting carrots and cabbage on at the same time as the spuds. Talk about killing off vitamins and flavour! Aunt Helene nudged me as I was about to say something. "Leave it," she hissed.

Before we left, Nana led me back into the room of a million and one dolls. She invited me to pick any doll I liked. I choose one from a pair of little monkeys in pale yellow waistcoats that matched their partly peeled bananas.

Nana said she had finished them in time to take home for Justin and Josh, but now the second monkey will go to Joseph, Uncle Trevor's little boy. I was given a pair of identical teddy bears for the twins instead.

I reckon she should make more of those witches on a broom like the one that hangs on Aunt Helene's porch that her friends like so much. Nana could cash in on the feminist wave Aunt Helene keeps rabbiting on about and get enough money to buy some modern kitchenware.

MONDAY

I'm at camp and it's amazing. As it was the first night, we had a red tin tea. I didn't know everyone was supposed to bring a tin of baked beans or spaghetti or tomatoes. Someone had brought saveloys that were thrown in the pot after a portion was taken out. I'm not sure I'd ever met a vegetarian before I came to this camp.

TUESDAY

A proper tea tonight. I'm in the girl's bunkhouse. Me and Monkey. I thought I'd be in with Aunt Helene. Grownups don't have to share rooms if they don't want to. One of the parent helpers says she snores. Her, that is. Not Aunt Helene.

WEDNESDAY

We all went to De Brett's hot pool. A girl there said I dress like a construction worker. So what? I'm not ashamed of my working-class background.

I know I will sweat and toil at my day-job as a roadie for a rock and roll band and I think it will do me good to do what my Dad calls honest labouring before I'm wealthy and famous. I couldn't do that in a pencil skirt and tailored jacket.

At home the key to my diary usually hangs on a shoelace around my neck along with the house key. Here, when I swim, I hide it in the button-down pocket of my board shorts. I can't afford to take any chances of my diary being read.

I explained about bringing only one pair of togs and Auntie Helene told them at my age what I wear to swim in shouldn't matter. I'm the youngest there and I'd much rather swim in shorts and a tank top.

THURSDAY

I've got a feeling Elise Thibault, the main tutor, is Madame Bovary, but I can't ask her outright, can I? If Kirstie were here, she'd know what to do. When I was reading my dialogue out loud, I kept getting it wrong because I was trying not to stare at her. Also I was trying not to laugh. Every time I looked at her the name Elise Thibault reminded me of a gangster holding a gun saying I'm going to release the bolt now and shoot.

I don't think Aunt Helene has noticed the resemblance between Madame Bovary and Elise Thibault. Just as well we're not sharing a room. What if I talk in my sleep? If I'm right, and Aunt Helene figures it out she will go ballistic like she did when she dragged me out of the gypsy house-truck.

FRIDAY

I've decided not to say anything to Elise Thibault about her being Madame Bovary. It could be embarrassing if I'm wrong as I hope to go to other writing camps in the future.

It's good for my career to be with future New Zealand playwrights, novelists and investigating journalists. Even when we do the same exercise we all come up with something different, and how you write doesn't seem to have anything to do with how old you are, but with who you are. I can't wait to see Kirstie again and tell her all about it.

SATURDAY

We had cleaned up by eleven this morning and said our goodbyes. I had everyone's address and promised to share camp photos and keep in touch.

No-one wanted to go. We left Taupo by midday and stopped at the Rangatiki pub on the way back to Napier and shared a bowl of spicy mince with chilli beans, salsa and a salad. Aunt Helene ordered mild but kept adding extra chilli sauce to her plate.

Once we got to Napier, we stayed at her friend Wanda's instead of Nana's. Wanda lives way up on the hill overlooking the city and there was almost nowhere to park. I had to wait back at the house with Wanda's fifteen-year-old daughter Rebecca when Aunt Helene went out for coffee and to shop with her friend. They were gone for ages.

Rebecca said, "They don't want us with them. Going shopping is a lie. They're heading for the private pools, the sort where you don't need swimwear."

"That's unlikely," I said, "because my aunt has brought dozens of swimsuits with her. Besides, she's had enough of hot pools this week to last a lifetime."

Rebecca laughed and called me a stupid kid with a lot to learn about life. Anyway, she had it all wrong because Aunt Helene returned with three brand new pairs of shorts and matching tank tops for me.

Later she asked me if I knew what discretion meant and then explained that what happens on tour stays on tour. Best not to talk too much about this and that because parents and grandparents might not understand.

I guess there'll be drinking and drugs when I'm a roadie driving a mega famous rock and roll band to gigs in a massive truck. There'll be lots of press about. I said, Hey, I'm Ross Jondell, personal manager and driver to the stars. A fly on the wall. I know how to keep my mouth shut.

Her friend Wanda shot me a look and asked, "Is that kid for real?" That was the only time she seemed to notice I was there. Before I settled down in the spare bed in Rebecca's room for the night, Aunt Helene pulled me aside and whispered that Sarah didn't need to know either we didn't stay at Nana's.

I reminded her it's good to have more than one friend and your best friend shouldn't get jealous when you have sleepovers at another friend's house. Then we linked pinkies together and whispered, "What happens on tour stays on tour."

I don't know why Sarah should be jealous, but if Aunt Helene wants us to keep this visit secret, that's fine by me. Aunt Helene kissed me and said thank you then crept off to Wanda's room.

SUNDAY

I was excited, but sad too, to be going back to Gisborne. Aunt said that feeling is called an anti-climax. You've been on a high, learning and experiencing different things. Then you find yourself plunged back into 'domesticity and the doldrums.' I do like how Aunt Helene explains things.

When she dropped me off she tapped her nose and wiggled her little finger, and called out, "Remember, Rosalyn, car troubles and your pinkie promise," and shot off. She couldn't wait to get home to Sarah, and I knew exactly how she felt. I can't wait to catch up with my best friend either.

Mum was keen to hear all about our travels. Dad butted in.

"So, I take it you didn't run into Wanda in Napier by any chance?"

I managed a blank stare and said, "Who?"

"Thank goodness," said Mum. "That'd throw a spanner into the works, wouldn't it, Steve?"

I trudged down the hall to my room and when I opened the door, what a surprise. The old bed had been replaced with a high bunk, but it's not single like the boys' – mine is a double with removable safety rails. Old furniture with stickers has go too, and instead of the Cinderella curtains I've got brand-new, grown-up drapes.

The floor's been sanded so the wood grain stands out and I've got two matching rugs. Far out! It's like deep down they know I'm going up in the world.

One more week of the holidays left. On Thursday night Kirstie is allowed to stay for a sleepover. So much to catch up on.

MONDAY
Slept most of the day

TUESDAY
I'm depressed. Hate being told what to do all the time. They treat me like a little kid. Can't wait for my real life to begin, with lots of freedom and enough money to do whatever I want.

WEDNESDAY
This morning Mum came into my room for a talk. She climbed up and sat on the ladder base end of the bunk, feet dangling, and asked me if I liked the improvements. Then she dropped her bombshell. They're renting my room out from time to time. So that's why it's been done up.

That figures!

I will get a pittance from the extra income, but must make a special effort to keep the room clean so it's ready at short notice. We'll see about that.

She says that we will offer weekend accommodation for 'out of towners' mostly young couples who come for events like surfing, or older ones for golf or bowls. On those nights I will sleep in the boy's room while the twins top and tail.

I said that I refuse to sleep on a mattress that's been piddled on, so Josh better get used to giving up his bed. The other thing is my room will occasionally now double as a space for visiting family and other guests.

Hell's teeth! I pointed out that lots of our relatives and the older golfers or bowlers will break their neck getting up onto the bed. Mum shook her head slowly and smiled. I hadn't even noticed. Dad has built it so when you take the middle portion of the poles out, it's only the same height as a regular double bed.

Mum will soon tire of cooking a full English breakfast with Tweedledee and Tweedledum pushing their cars round and round the kitchen table.

THURSDAY

When I told Kirstie about the deal with my new bed, she said the words I'm looking for are 'ulterior motive' and 'Kiwi ingenuity.'

Kirstie read my diary and questioned me about Madame Bovary. I said that Elise Thibault's Canadian accent and her figure is the same, but the hair is different. Kirstie thinks that a wig could explain all that, and the word she says I'm looking for is physique not figure.

Thibault's an unfortunate name, even if it's in the top twenty most popular French-Canadian surnames. Now I can't get it out of my head – it's weird for a writer whose first name is Elise to have a surname linked to every day plumbing and general maintenance like unscrewing a nut to release the bolt.

Kirstie says we'll find a poster of Madame Bovary doing the rounds of A&P shows. We will compare this with the image of Elise Thibault in one the many magazines she writes for. I don't know why I didn't think of that first.

When I'm a hard-nosed investigative journalist, Kirstie can do my research from my New York office. I will need a Kiwi flatmate.

We were sitting up at either end of my new high bed with our Monkey and Curious George when Dad marched in saying it was late and to keep the racket down. He turned the light off. Dad said he did knock first, but we were so rowdy we didn't hear.

It's a good thing the olds don't know where I hide my diary because I have no privacy. Now they've invested in it, they barge in and behave as if my room is theirs.

FRIDAY

I'm sorting my camp photos and putting them into an album. I've contacted Jessica. She's the ten-year-old from Hastings.

SATURDAY

Mum goes back to work today, half-days on a Saturday as usual. Because it's still school holidays we're allowed to stay home instead of going into town on the bus. Dad's headed out for a couple of hours.

Kirstie, Lori and Jennifer are here helping with the twins. Kirstie even brought Jimmy over.

Mrs Milton has dropped over three times already. Now she's sitting on our porch. I bet Dad's arranged for her to spy on us. By the time he got back, Isobel was also here. He says the place looks like a day-care centre and that we could have asked, instead of scoffing every cracker in the house.

We are stocked up for house guests. I hope he's not getting any more money-making ideas.

SUNDAY

School term starts again tomorrow. Isobel, Jennifer and Lori are planning on running away. They counted their combined pocket money and only had enough to buy a few lollies.

When they've got enough funds they'll leave town together. Kirstie and I have been sworn to secrecy.

MONDAY

What can I say about the first school day back? Ho-hum. Except there's a new boy in the senior class.

Callum talks Scottish, which hardly sounds like English. He wears a kilt. That's good news for me, because he's a boy wearing a skirt. Now I can wear my brand-new board shorts to school and be a girl wearing trousers! Ha ha ha!

TUESDAY

Charlie Davis stole a bunch of bananas off the fruit and veg truck that sometimes parks outside the school. He ran back through the playground with the truck owner chasing after him with a machete. We got into trouble for laughing. Mr Morrissey made Charlie give the fruit back and say sorry.

WEDNESDAY

Dad hushed us because he was listening to the radio at breakfast. They were talking about a man who played for Phillip Wrigley, owner of the Chicago Baseball team, who had died at age eighty-two.

"What's baseball?" asked Josh.

Mum said, "That's the same man who founded the

chewing gum empire. He's to blame for all the chewing gum stuck everywhere, especially in children's hair."

The Bible in School's lesson didn't make any sense as usual. Kirstie says she hates it when they march dullards into the school to teach kids. I agreed with her.

"They should leave it to the professionals to mess up our minds. At least they're paid properly to do it."

THURSDAY

First writers' meeting since camp. Aunt Helene and I stopped at the library because I wanted to check out some writing magazines and pick up another book on Bangladeshi slums.

FRIDAY

I was about to walk out the front door in my new shorts Aunt Helene bought in Napier when Mum sent me back inside to change into a skirt.

"A dress would be nice for a change," she said. "You never seem to look like the other girls."

When I told her about Callum wearing a kilt she said, "That's different. That's a cultural exception." Apparently, if I start wearing shorts, this will 'challenge the school dress code.'

Why do adults always say that? It's all an excuse. My parents don't want to be called to the school to discuss me or they're scared I'll start a revolution. I happen to have the sort of parents who don't believe in anything enough to march for it. I told Mum so.

"You can't rage against convention, Rosalyn, or fly in the face of school rules. No point swimming against the tide."

And Dad chipped in, "Little by little wins the day. Rome wasn't built in a week, you know. Softly, softly, catchee monkey."

I don't even know what that means and I wonder if they adopted me and haven't got round to confessing. Otherwise how could I have ended up with such conventional parents?

SATURDAY

I took the writing magazines over to Kirstie's to show her Elise Thibault's photo. She said it doesn't prove anything. We need a poster of the gypsy fair or some other public event Madame Bovary attends. Then we can compare the two and decide if it's the same woman.

SUNDAY

We were walking along the pipes when Jennifer slipped and fell in the mud. Good job she didn't fall from the giant sewerage pipe into the creek. She might have got cholera and died. I hope she hasn't caught something else. That mud was smelly.

I ran home to get some dry clothes, so Jennifer could change in the bushes. Isobel was thinking up a story to explain away the muddy clothing.

We're not allowed to play there. We made Jennifer stop whimpering and walked quickly along the railway lines to where McKenzie Street backs on to it.

Luckily Lori's olds who live on that side at number nine are hardly ever outside, or her mother would tell mine that she saw us go past. It's like living in a police state sometimes.

MONDAY

Mr Morrissey is always saying, "No question is too stupid," but today as usual Charlie Davis proved him wrong.

What happened was teacher told us this blind girl from America is coming to our school for a week. That explains why he's been reading us the Helen Keller story.

I immediately wondered if our visitor might bring her seeing-eye dog then remembered quarantine. And it would be difficult to bring a seeing-eye dog to another country at the bottom of the world. Much better for her dog, if she even has one, to be left at home. I'm glad I kept my mouth shut.

That was sensible because Sam Shaw asked if the blind girl will have someone beside her to draw signs on her hand. Mr Morrissey explained Marcia is blind not deaf. I hope Mr Morrissey noticed that at least Sam has been paying attention during the reading of the Helen Keller story.

It's no surprise Charlie Davis was sent to the Principal's office with a note though. He asked how blind people can tell when they've wiped their bottoms properly. Except he wasn't as polite as that.

He used a four-letter word and talked about the state of the used toilet paper. I'm not easily shocked and he was disgusting. Mr Morrissey stopped him half way. Most of the class were laughing. Most of my classmates are so immature.

I've never seen Mr Morrissey so quiet. He stood with his mouth open for some time, as though he couldn't think of what to say.

"Blind people are no different from the rest of us, Charlie. Except for eyesight."

He picked up his pen and jotted something down.

"Now take this to Mr Collinson's office, please," and handed him the note.

Charlie didn't come back. Later, he tapped on our classroom window. We were told to completely ignore him. Not easy. He was making funny faces. He should think seriously about becoming a clown. No. You couldn't have him anywhere near children. Gran would give his mouth a good washing out with soap.

About half an hour later I nudged Lori and pointed with my head. Charlie was trudging around the far end of the playground with a trash bag picking up rubbish.

TUESDAY

Her name is Marcia. Marcia Van der Plank, and she's from Texas. She's in Year 6 and she's African-American. She's eleven because they don't start school until they are six years old in America.

She's travelling with her aunt, who's as posh as, and who organised Marcia's stay along with the Education Board and the Foundation for the Blind in both countries.

The aunt gave us a brief greeting then rushed off to drink tea – or coffee more likely, being American – in the staffroom and entertain the teachers.

After Marcia finished telling us about herself, Ben Marks asked her if she knew the Lone Ranger. It's hard to tell what blind people are thinking because their eyes don't show surprise.

Mr Morrissey said, "Yes, like Marcia the Lone Ranger was indeed from Texas, but Ben should remember only Marcia is real." Then he added, "Class, sensible questions from now on, please."

Marcia told us a thing the blind do with echo. I've forgotten the word. She explained that it's by bouncing sounds off walls and things that she knows her way around. At the base of her white stick is a ball she rolls while she's walking.

Marcia will do the same school curriculum as everyone else. No, I forgot. She's excused from art classes. When she was younger, she had a teacher aide, but for the past few years she's used a braille keyboard.

She can read and write and even do maths with it. At her own school she can recognise every pupil and teacher from their voices alone. Awesome.

She even rides a bike at home in her own community, a tandem, though it's sad she can never steer it, or won't ever drive a truck. If I knew for certain I'd never get to drive a digger or any earthmoving machinery when I grew up, I would be totally depressed.

WEDNESDAY

Whew. Jennifer didn't get sick from falling into the mud by the sewerage ponds on Sunday. We'd have been in real trouble then cos we're not supposed to play there. I kept an eye on her and she did run to the loo a few times, but she wasn't throwing up or drinking heaps. What a relief.

Since Marcia came I'm scared stiff of going blind. When I open up couldn't my eyes first thing in the morning I'm always pleased I can still see.

Aunt Helene told me once that she knows a man who'd been to Homai College, the school for the blind in Auckland. He got mad because people didn't realise he was from Vanuatu. This is because his skin is so pale. She explained that albino people like Tomasi have inherited a genetic disorder that results in a lack of pigmentation.

This explains the pale skin. It affects their eyes and albino people's eyes and skin are sensitive to the sun. Aunt Helene's friend sounds interesting. I'd like to interview him someday.

Aunt Helene says Tomasi had low vision from birth. Marcia, on the other hand, was born completely blind. She says I need to realise that the non-sighted have 'altered expectations' to sighted kids. They grow up knowing they'll never drive. They're not sad about it. Not at all.

I hope she's right.

The entire school has been sent home with a notice about head lice. We've been told we must do the treatment together for it to work. What will Marcia think of us? Of all the schools, she had to visit ours when this happened. How shaming.

Though Mum says there's no shame in it, no shame at all. That children attract nits is a well-known fact and for some reason the little critters prefer a kid's head to an adult, and the cleaner the better. It makes no sense.

She read our notices, then phoned Dad to get the nit treatment Derbac on his way home from work.

After tea she sent us to run around outside because the stuff on our heads was so yucky and smelly. The Davis kids across the road were lined up in order of size. Charlie Davis was staring right at me, but probably didn't recognise me with my hair all gummed up and piled on top.

His Mum was pouring something on their heads. Dad said its kerosene. It was how they killed nits in his day. You can pass out from the fumes. That's why they're doing it outside.

When Molly Davis yelled, she got a slap and her Mum shouted, "You little wimp. Shut up or I'll give you something to cry over, you sooky bubba. Shut up, I said, or you'll get your father's belt on your backside."
She didn't say backside and now I know where Charlie got his foul mouth from.

I hope the Davis grown-ups don't light up around them till that kerosene's washed out. Dad says it's probably stinging Molly's scalp. He remembers that feeling only too well. I must ask Napier Nana about that, though she'll probably deny it.

After Mum washed off the stinky shampoo, she sat us down with old towels around our shoulders and went through our hair with a special comb. Justin started blubbering and Dad said if he has to go through all this again, he'll shave the twins' heads. Oh my God, they'll be like little old men.

If I was bald I'd never step out of the house again. It's times like this I'm pleased I'm not a boy.

THURSDAY

For writing group tonight, we had to write a descriptive paragraph about loud sounds. Problem is, we're not allowed to use the word loud. It's harder than it seems.

I've left it to the last minute because of Marcia, and because of the time it took last night to treat the head lice.

CAUGHT IN A STORM
BY ROZ JONDELL
AGED 9

We crouched in the corner of the cave. Some of the smaller girls started sobbing at a high volume. Outside, the trees creaked, and the wind screamed.

The storm as it raged was deafening. It was so noisy we could hardly hear Brown Owl leading us in taps and other guiding songs. We were so happy to be saved we clapped our hands…

What? I must fill in that missing word before tonight.

As we were leaving her house, Aunt Helene nearly tripped over her cat as it circled round and round mewing.

"Confounded rowdy feline." She pushed it away with her foot.

"I'll feed you after I drop Roz at her writing group."

I patted 'the rowdy feline' and smiled. I'd found the missing word in the nick of time as the oldies say.

We were so happy to be saved we clapped our hands for the rescuers and added some rowdy cheers.

FRIDAY

I was dropped home at seven as usual. I walked in to find my parents in the middle of a fight. I hope this doesn't mean the beginning of a divorce.

I knew I shouldn't have mentioned yesterday that Madison O'Brien, the twins' classmate, had obviously not had any hair treatment. Perhaps it wouldn't have mattered, except I said it to the boys who then told Mum the O'Brien girls turned up with their usual tangled bird's nests.

"Be reasonable, Steve," she said as she burned toast for our breakfast. "The O'Briens probably couldn't afford it. Ye gods, it was an expense we could have done without this week."

"But there's no flipping point unless everyone does the hair treatment, Esmé. If even only one family won't play ball, the kids will be back to square one within hours."

"I know that, Steve. I was just saying."

"They could always use something else, surely."

"Oh, so now you're recommending your Mum's old standby, kerosene, eh?"

"No… Still, remember what the Navy says, any port in a storm. And don't start criticising my mother. She managed as best she could. She was a widow on a shoestring income, don't forget."

"As was mine. Don't you dare bring our mothers into this. Both of them were strong, resourceful women battling difficult times. Stop changing the focus. We're talking about now, Steve, not then."

"Esmé, don't you get it? Nothing changes. Every generation ends up dealing with nits. Those who can't afford the proper stuff should use something else."

"Not kerosene, it's barbaric."

"So if you were an O'Brien kid with no other option, would you prefer kerosene or making yourself unpopular by sharing your nits with your classmates?"

"I don't think I'm that keen about being held down to have kerosene poured over my head. But I suppose you think that's all right."

I don't think they even noticed I was home. I had to interrupt in the end so Mum could sort out our school lunches. Dad did his stomp around the house like he always does when he and Mum have words.

Kirstie and I gave Marcia the school tiki tour during the lunch break. I could tell Marcia was bored by being buddied up with Françoise in Year 6 today. Probably the most boring kid ever born.

Everyone trailed after us and I felt like a tour guide showing a celebrity some famous house and garden.

I apologised about our school head lice situation. She chuckled and said we're not alone with that problem; it happens in American schools too. Is that why Marcia has dozens of tight little plaits tipped with coloured beads?

Rowan's hair is covered in grease. Her mother doesn't believe in sudden death, even for nits. She says oil loosens the eggs so they comb out easily.

I'm keeping quiet about that or my parents will divorce for sure when Dad brings home five litres of soya bean oil. Like The Cat in the Hat Comes Back with the ring around the bath. My mother would have a meltdown over oil on our towels and pillowcases.

As we walked around one of the kids shouted, "Hello, Marcia, it's Tracey here from Year Four. Do you want to feel my face?"

Kirstie reminded her Marcia is blind, not deaf and so there was no need to yell. In fact, she said, her hearing is probably more finely tuned than ours. Besides, the blind don't go around feeling faces. That's only in the movies."

Kirstie does like telling people things they don't want to know.

Gillian Nikora wanted to know if Marcia had seen that movie about the blind black singer (no one could remember his name) and how he learned to match up his socks by colour.

And that cheeky bugger Simon Gordon tried to make a joke.

"Maybe Marcia went, Gillian, but she certainly didn't see it, silly."

I'm glad to say nobody laughed.

When the crowds died down I reminded Marcia how much I'd like to be her companion when we're both grown up, touring the world educating the ignorant.

"I'll drive the mobile rig," I promised. "Accommodation and an office on giant wheels. Won't that be cool?"

I shouldn't have offered to ghostwrite her book though.

"I'm perfectly capable of writing my own story in Braille without assistance," she told me, and I back-tracked immediately.

"I was thinking more of helping with a cover and the layout of the book side of things. Details like white or cream for the paper and what font worked best."

I stopped myself in time from adding, "The things sighted people do."

Marcia reminded me she's two years older and might have started her travels before I could join her. However, she did make me tell her my phone number over and over until she had memorised it.

SATURDAY

I was hoping Marcia and her host family might come into the Americano. I told her lunch was on me. I did exaggerate a bit when I hinted Mum co-owned the café. Maybe it's better that she didn't turn up. I hadn't asked how many to expect and I might have run out of pocket money. That could have been embarrassing.

When we got home I got a phone call. Marcia said she was sorry she couldn't make it, but would I like to come to Wainui Beach on the outskirts of Gisborne where she and her aunt were staying.

"Say ten tomorrow morning," she drawled.

Would I? I couldn't wait! Me and my family were all invited for morning tea. I wanted my aunt to meet her aunt.

"Thanks, Marcia, that sounds great. I'll ask and get back to you."

And here was me thinking she was mad at me for suggesting I could ghostwrite her story for her. Whew!

SUNDAY

Dad agreed we could go to morning tea at Marcia's, but he didn't think it would be polite to bring along an additional aunt, even when I tried to explain the two aunts needed to 'brainstorm and network' future tours.

"Network. That's a new word for you, isn't it?"

Dad raised his eyebrows in that funny way he does when he's not taking me seriously.

"Rosalyn," he said, "You don't need to be planning your career just yet. You've still another year left in primary school, remember."

So, sadly, Aunt Helene didn't come. The olds don't get it. Aunt Helene is already my agent and manager. But they promised to only stay for a cup of tea, though, then take the boys down to the beach and pick me up later.

When we got there, Dad recognised the house. It was a new-build and his firm won the plumbing contract about three years ago. Turned out the host father and Dad went to youth club together years ago, and Mum took up his wife's offer of a tour of the house before we sat down for morning tea.

It's the first time we'd tasted pumpkin pie, but I didn't let on. I thanked Ms Van der Plank and said it was the most delicious pie I'd ever tasted and the mix of spices was perfect. When they realised it was vegetables, the twins screwed up their noses and gobbled up the brownies.

Marcia's aunt looks much younger than mine. I guess it's the up-market grooming and clothing style.

Eventually we took the private track past waving toe toe that led from the beach house to the water's edge – Marcia and me, the two boys who lived there and Josh and Justin.

"Don't go too far," Dad called. "Stay within sight and watch those boys near water?"

"Are they still on the deck drinking coffee and stuffing their faces with pie?" Marcia asked once we'd gone far enough down.

"Yep. Grown-ups love to hang out together with no kids around. It's a real Kiwi thing."

"I think you'll find its pretty much the same everywhere, Roz."

Turns out as we talked Marcia was never mad at me. She likes my energy and motivation. Her little sister's my age and is nothing like me. Sometimes Marcia talks like one of those American books on 'self-development and affirmation' that Aunt Helene's friend Sarah is always buying her.

"I'm just a normal Kiwi kid," I told her, "brought up with a can-do attitude and No. 8 wire solutions."

I had to explain about No. 8 wire to Marcia, and she went on.

"I hadn't even thought of a promotional tour until you suggested it. We ought to stay in touch. I reckon we'll end up touring America together, with or without the aunts."

I gently reminded her that we can't rely on them forever. Marcia doesn't know what ageing looks like. She only goes by voices. I once heard an old tape recording of Gran when she was Mum's age. Her voice still sounds exactly the same today. Marcia can't guess someone's age by looking. How could she?

"My aunt's nearly forty already," I told her. "I'm not sure she'll be fit enough to travel by the time we're grown-up. We need to develop independence because one day, sadly, our aunts will be gone."

Turns out Marcia's aunt has had a facelift. She openly admitted it, said Mum. That explains everything. But nothing surprises me about her. I get the impression she's wealthy.

MONDAY

The school seems empty now Marcia Van der Plank isn't here. She's going to Australia next, staying in the outback.

Blind people in aboriginal territory don't get a seeing-eye guide dog. Those dogs are expensive to train, much too valuable to be eaten by crocodiles.

TUESDAY

Our next exercise for writers' group is to write something that describes touch and smell. After tea I read Dead Cat to the olds.

Josh inspired this poem because he keeps asking me to cut up this cat we pass on the way home from school. That stinky dead cat is only about four doors down. So close I'm surprised we can't smell it from our house.

I'll copy the poem out here.

DEAD CAT

By Roz Jondell - Aged 9

In the gutter.
I tap him. No movement.
He's stiff as a bored.
Maggots crawl through teeth that
once chewed on mice. The mouth is
silent that once said meow.
I turn him over with my stick.
His bloated tummy moves as if he
still lives and breathes.
He stinks, like a hardworking plumber
who hasn't had time for a shower.
I pause.
Is it a boy or a girl cat with kittens?
I take out my pocket knife and hold my nose.
Then ring the SPCA to collect
the unborn kittens.
I'm a lifesaver.

The End

They both say, "Very nice, dear. Keep up the good work." Nice? They don't get what writing is all about, do they? Then Mum puts out her hand and reads it through. She points out bored is a verb, and board is the noun I wanted, and counts the words. (95.)

Dad mutters something about stinking plumbers taking showers. Mum smiles sweetly at him and says, "Yes, that part really speaks to the audience."

And Josh asks if we can slice open the real dead gutter cat when we're going to school. I'm starting to worry about that boy. He likes messy smelly stuff.

They're only five, the twins, and can't read yet. Kids that age have no idea where inspiration comes from. I don't expect either of them will ever be able to recognise great literature. Like others with talent I'll have to accept the lonely fact that my family, apart from Aunt Helene, won't ever truly appreciate me.

WEDNESDAY
The Bible in Schools lady sent me to the Principal today. I was supposed to go straight to his office without reading the note, but nipped into the toilet first. I was disobedient and argumentative according to her.

"Things have well and truly come to a head with Mrs Jolly, haven't they, Rosalyn?"

Mr Collin's eyes twinkled, and he turned a laugh into a cough when I told him, "There's nothing jolly about that woman."

Then he put on his teacher face and sent me to the staffroom to wash up the cups and dishes.

"Then come back and sit on the bench outside my office, Rosalyn, and write about a character in the Bible."

I chose Thomas. When I handed it in, he gave me a note to take home. He suggested I be allowed to join those excused from religious instruction. No Mrs Jolly, but I'll be stuck in a class to do set work along with atheists and Seventh Day Adventists.

Oh, and Lori, who's excused too because she's a Catholic.

THURSDAY
I had this dream where I was a Russian spy like the one in The Man from Uncle, tall and handsome with stubble

on my chin. I was smoking a cigar and celebrating with a British spy in a warehouse. We'd just saved the Soviet Union from some disaster. Dreams are always mixed-up.

In my dream I was about my parents' age. If dreams do turn out true, I'm destined for a long life. If Elise Thibault is Madame Bovary I might ask her what it means.

Kirstie wanted to know why I had saved Russia instead of Britain. She likes Napoleon Solo in The Man from Uncle. I prefer Ilya Kuryakin and in the dream my hair is blond like his.

Kirstie says being a man in the dream means I have a deep-seated fear of menopause. Thank you, Madame Kirstie Jarrett!

I still don't know what menopause is! I once asked my Aunt Julie when I over-heard her and Mum talking about someone they knew who had it. She laughed and said it means 'a pause between men.'

She added, "You'll know all about it if you live long enough, Rosalyn."

Kirstie says facial stubble is a problem for menopausal women. She knows someone who had radiation treatment to cure it. Her jaw went chalky and later fell off.

Tonight when I read Dead Cat to the writing group one of the older boys pointed out if the cat had been dead long enough for maggots to breed the kittens would be dead.

I felt like kicking myself and was sort of embarrassed because he was right. Silly mistake. I hadn't thought the logic through properly I guess. It's awful being the youngest sometimes.

Seamus stood up for me. He said that my poem was a valiant attempt to employ creative use of poetic licence. He told us it's important to put our work out there. I wrote notes of what else he said.

Once our work is in the public domain it's important to learn to deal with negative constructive criticism. Authors must develop a thick skin. Some writers give up early because they lack the courage. To be published is to open ourselves up to criticism that isn't always kind.

"Treat all feedback as a learning curve. Here at Junior Writers we provide a safe space to practice."

Then he said exactly the same thing as Mum and Dad when I read Dead Cat to them in the first place. Déjà vu again.

"Keep up the good work, Roz."

After Junior Writers I had tea with Aunt Helene and Sarah. I slept in the double bed as usual. Sarah seems to be there all the time these days. I'm surprised she's still sharing Aunt's bedroom and hasn't taken over the spare room.

"When she does," I told Aunt Helene, "I won't mind sleeping in the lounge on a mattress. Long as it's not a camp stretcher."

FRIDAY

I told our parents that Josh *still* keeps nagging me to cut open the dead cat on the way to and from school. Plus it's starting to stink real bad now. Dad says he will take a spade to bury it in the weekend.

Mum phoned the council, who told her it's not an animal control issue because a dead cat is neither a runaway horse or a vicious dog. When she put down the phone she used some four-letter words in front of the twins. I put my hands over Josh's ears to show her how shocked and disappointed I was.

"Aunt Helene is the only hope for this family," I said.

Lucky we were about to leave the house because Mum turned bright red and l thought she was going to jump up and slap me.

"Leave it, Esmé," Dad said. "I'll put the jug on."

I saw Rowan at interval. She's in the next class up, the one Charlie Davis should be in. I told her I'm also joining the group excused from religious class.

She's the only child of a single mother. Rowan says they are Wiccan and reckons all world religions are patriarchal, not just the Christian sects. I didn't understand what she's talking about. I should be learning lots on Wednesday mornings for a change.

She asked me if I was related to Helene Jondell. It seems Rowan's mother belongs to the same women's group as my aunt.

At lunch-time it was cold sitting on the forms outside the classroom eating our packed lunches. I know American kids have indoor dining, hot meals and dinner ladies. I've seen that on TV.

Today they brought around the hot chocolate for those of us who'd paid and brought our mugs from home. I was rubbing my cold knees. I wish we were allowed to wear long trousers. Maybe I will get a scholarship and move to America. Then I could wear whatever I like to school.

SATURDAY

At breakfast Mum explained to the boys that although it's not OK to swear sometimes even grown-ups make mistakes. That she was sorry for using bad language yesterday.

"You're less likely to use bad language, aren't you, Mum, if you develop a good vocabulary like Aunt Helene's." I glanced at Dad. "I have never heard your sister swear. Ever."

Later I remembered that one time I overheard her at Nana's. Dad pushed his breakfast away.

"I've had enough of this palaver, Esmé. I'll leave you to sort it out."

And he stalked out to the shed without taking his plate to the sink. How rude. Mum had gone to the trouble making her French bread and omelette speciality, too, his favourite.

I told her it was very, very tasty and to prove it I ate Dad's leftovers. Her feelings must be hurt.

"Put your feet up, Mum, and I'll make you a nice cup of coffee."

She said nothing, just shook her head and pointed at the door. I left the room.

SUNDAY

There was a photograph of Desmond Burton in the weekend paper scowling over a stack of op shop coats. He's mad as hell because someone from the Salvation Army took his old clothes away when he was at the bottle store and left a bundle of clean, second-hand coats.

Desmond wants his back, with the rat piss and poo on them. His pet rat and her babies were in the pocket of his favourite coat. He wants to know what's happened to his rodent pals.

"Dad, can we go down to the Wag-a-Tail pet shop and I'll buy him a pet rat in a cage," I said. "I've got enough pocket money put aside."

He stared me straight in the face.

"If you ever go anywhere near that man, my girl, I will whack your backside so hard you won't be able to sit down for a week."

I was shocked.

"That sort of violent statement will reflect badly on you when I do my big expose on Desmond in under ten years."

"Look, Rosalyn," he scoffed, "you've got a kind heart, but

Burton will be a distant memory by then. Besides, you'll probably be off to uni or serving an apprenticeship in the trades or in the military or driving a truck somewhere."

Dad knows me well, but not that well. I will remember to interview Desmond Burton. He's in my long-term writing goals.

Then Dad said, "The older we get, the more we realise how little we knew when we were young."

I wonder about him sometimes when he comes up with that kind of stupid stuff. I'm young and I know a lot.

MONDAY

There's an appointment card for Justin to see a urologist. I don't know how long they've been hiding it from me.

Mum doesn't think it's necessary, says there's nothing to worry about. Everyone's been telling her to get Justin seen to, just in case. His appointment's on Wednesday, nine thirty. He's not going to school in the morning.

Kirstie says Justin may end up with a catheter. That's a urine bag my parents will have to empty every day. I feel sorry for him. How will he go swimming? I wish I hadn't been so mean about him wetting himself.

"Grandpa has one of those piddling bags," said Lori.

"My uncle had his prostrate cut out," said Isobel, "and something went wrong."

"The only real threat to a child that young is the general anaesthetic."

Kirstie's aunt is a nurse who works in the operating room and is always telling her scary stories.

I'm beginning to worry about my own prostate now. I wonder where it is? And it'd be so sad to have a brain-damaged little brother. He'll have to go to the special school if they bungle the surgery and he ends up a vegetable.

There's been a few cases in the newspaper now I think about it. I'm beginning to appreciate how much I'll need my friends in a time of crisis.

When we walked home after school and that evening I was especially kind to poor little Justin.

TUESDAY

Mr Morrissey told me off for not paying attention in class. I told him I was worried sick about my little brother, but he still made me hand in my maths book. I had only answered three out of twenty questions.

At interval while Josh played tag with Lori's brother, I spent some quality time with Justin. We need to build good memories, Justin and me.

"Are you all right, dear?" asked Miss Downes.

How could I be? She ought to know better She knows Justin won't be in her class tomorrow. Or possibly forever.

The subject of operations has been banned at the dinner table. Dad got mad at me, and I don't blame him. He's worried too. I've been sent to bed early. I don't mind. They also need to spend quality time with the boys tonight.

Josh. I picture us walking hand in hand to school. Just the two of us. Such a lonely image. I'm crying. I have no-one to talk to right now except Monkey, and you, dear diary.

WEDNESDAY

I hugged Justin so hard before Josh and me left for school. I can't remember how many times I told him I loved him.

"Hurry up," said Mum. "Go now or you'll be late."

I hugged her, too. She was doing such a good job of hiding her fear. Josh really has no idea. It was like déjà vu walking to school holding Josh's hand, the two of us, like I imagined it last night.

The bell rang. I didn't want to leave Josh alone in the infant room with Justin's absence such a big gap. It'll be hard for us to recover. Miss Downes was a bit harsh, I think.

"Hurry up, Rosalyn. Go to your own class or you'll get a late mark."

Déjà vu again. Oh, how I wanted to poke out my tongue. That woman has no imagination.

I was hanging up my coat and bag in the corridor when Mr Morrissey called out, "Hurry up, Rosalyn Jondell. You'd better have a good excuse for being late."

Another uncaring teacher and more déjà vu.

By lunchtime Justin was back at school. He said the doctor pulled down his underpants to take a look. Justin's underpants, not the doctor's. He was wearing gloves, but his hands were cold. The doctor's hands, not Justin's.

When she got home, Mum sent the boys outside with a chocolate bar each. We sat at the table together and ate half a packet of Mellopuffs with a jug of hot chocolate.

"The school rang me," she said. "We have a few things to clear up."

Firstly, Justin was never in danger. I was so relieved. Second, he's absolutely normal and will grow out of it. Some boys take longer than others. Third, in the meantime we will use a star chart with rewards for dry beds and pants at school.

"So you can stop worrying, Rosalyn, and turning everything into a drama. Here, there's a couple of Mellowpuffs left."

She pushed the packet of biscuits over and went out to call the boys in.

THURSDAY

Mum is wrong about Josh being more emotionally robust

than Justin. He's having a major meltdown. He wants a star chart just like Justin's and he's threatening to wet his pants, too, so he can get rewards. Why didn't Mum tell the doctor Justin had a twin?

If I was the doctor, I'd have sent Justin to a special bedwetters' camp until he learnt to be dry like the rest of the family.

I'm published! In Letters to the Editor in the local paper. I can't wait to show the others at writers' group tonight.

"Esmé, listen to this ignoramus," Dad said at breakfast, and he read my letter out.

"How heartless are the people of Gisborne to take away an old man's coats. Do they think coats that are clean will comfort him in these cold nights under the Old Colonial Bridge when the poor man is obviously grieving over the loss of his family of rats. Shame he has no-one but them to love him.

"If someone has a drinking problem or is homeless, he should be helped. I've been a resident of Gisborne for nearly ten years now. I'm sad and ashamed to live in such a city."

"Who's it by, dear? Do we know them?"

"Some drongo named Ross Bovary."

"Ten years. He knows nothing about Desmond Burton. Nothing, I say. If he doesn't like it here, he should go back to where he came from."

"I've got a good mind to tell him we tried to help Desmond Burton back in my youth club days, Esmé. Held a car wash to raise funds to buy him a wooden packing crate to sleep in. We school boys even dragged it down the riverbank for him."

"I remember that. Didn't it burn down?"

"Yes, arson, I think."

"No, Steve, he set it alight when he was smoking in bed." She picked up the newspaper and read the letter again. "You should write a reply to the editor... No. What about..."

And she nodded towards me.

"What about asking Rosalyn to write it for you?" I didn't like how she was smiling. "It would be good practice for you, dear, and you did say you wanted to write an article about him."

"Your mother's right, Rosalyn. What a good start for your writing career."

I got the newspaper cutting when I said I needed it for research. When I showed it to my friends, I didn't mention what the olds had said, but it did make me think.

I didn't share my publishing success at writers' group after all. Instead I waited until Sarah left the room and showed it to Aunt Helene.

"Read this. What do you think of it?"

She took it, and smiled. "I saw that in the paper at breakfast. You'll have to think up a less obvious nom de plume, won't you?"

And then explained what a nom de plume is.

FRIDAY

A wet day. We sloshed to school in our gumboots and rainwear and changed into our slippers. Two grandmothers knitting for us comes in handy.

We had interval and lunch in the classroom. When anyone goes to the toilet block, there are two golf umbrellas in buckets outside each class. The teachers are getting sick of putting the umbrellas up and down. I'm sick of smelly feet.

SATURDAY

Still pouring down.

"You and the twins are going nowhere in this weather," said Dad.

"Why can't we go on the bus?"

"You can't clog up Mum's diner on a busy wet day. The twins can watch cartoons as it's too wet to go out."

I'm making two carts out of beer crates and pram wheels. It's the simple classic design Dad showed me and should be easy-peasy to make. One long plank and two crossbars for the axles. One fixed, one swivel. Rope steering. Beer-crate at rear.

Oh, and a basic wooden lever braking system, I should have it all finished by the time Mum's home. Dad said he will lend a hand if I need it, but I won't.

It took me ages to hand saw through the plank for the rear axle. I kept checking the instructions on the blackboard, measured twice, cut once. I ruined the first and when I was nearly done deliberately broke it. Bad idea. Then I had to start all over again.

I begged Dad to let me use the table-saw.

"Put in the hard graft, Rosalyn. It'll be worth it. You need to practise standing directly over the intended cut."

After lunch when Mum came home I showed her the results of my morning's work. The rear axle crossbar was nailed to the main plank body. I think she was impressed.

I used the hand drill to make the swivel hole in the front axle and fitted the bolt and tightened with spanner. I wasn't allowed to use the electric drill and I had two more holes to drill for the rope.

The end result did favour the right-hand side a little, but Dad says that won't matter for a kid's cart running at slow speed. What does he mean slow speed? Doesn't he realise how fast I can move.

He's re-working a quality rimu cabinet. Such a tightwad. He'd rather mess with that tatty old furniture than buy new.

Mum called us in for tea. Dad says we can finish the first cart tomorrow and make a start on the second. Whew.

SUNDAY

An old man came over with a horse float trailer early this morning. He loaded the rimu cabinet on it with Dad's help. A number of five, ten and twenty dollar bills changed hands and Dad shoved them in his pocket.

Shortly after that, he took the work van out on a job. That's the worst thing about being a plumber he reckons. When there's been steady rain the drains clog up.

I looked at the list of tools I'm allowed to use without supervision. Hammer, hand drill and hand saw. I can also use the plane, vice, sandpaper and nails. Dad has the table-saw plug locked up in a little box he's made.

He says you can never be too careful with table or skill-saws. Even if that random person wandered in from the street wanting to use it, I wouldn't know where the key is anyway.

I hate admitting defeat. I did want to finish that first cart, but I'll have to wait until Dad's back.

What a weird afternoon. No more cart making. When Dad returned, we got picked up for the movies with my cousins. I wanted to go to Kirstie's instead, but Mum said I couldn't come home before 5pm. So there I was squished in Aunt Julie's van with all the kids.

I still don't know if my parents went out, or if they stayed home. When we pulled up in our driveway Mum said, "Oh, back so soon?" She and Dad were smiling. I expect they were glad to see us. It must be boring when they've only got each other for company.

Aunt Julie gave Dad a big sloppy kiss.

"Happy birthday, little brother. Did you have a good afternoon?"

Dad winked at Mum and nodded, and the three olds giggled in that stupid way grown-ups sometimes do. I'd forgotten it's Dad's birthday this week.

MONDAY

The minute I saw Mr Morrissey in his good jacket and tie, and Mrs Girton in that dress she only wears on special days, I knew the teachers were up to something.

Turns out the school inspectors are due in. Mr Morrissey had some new stuff written up on the board. 'Think outside the square' and 'Creativity begins with asking questions.'

The inspector sat at the back and never smiled once. She wore a grey tailored suit with a plain white blouse. It looked good on her. Professional. I must ask Mum to buy me a suit.

Again.

Mr Morrissey got me up the front to read my latest story. I left my houndstooth workman's jersey on my chair. I hope the inspector noticed my wardrobe choice is similar to hers.

At interval I saw Mr Morrissey slip Noel Perkins a barley sugar. He didn't have his hand down his pants all morning. Noel that is. Not Mr Morrissey.

TUESDAY

That stupid doctor. Josh hasn't wet his pants like he threatened, but now he has a star chart for keeping his side of their room tidy. Justin has managed to stay dry though.

Justin also wants another star chart, otherwise he won't bother tidying up his side. Josh started crying. He says it's not fair if Justin has two star charts while he ` has only one.

I'm glad Kirstie, Lori and I have sworn never to have kids. If I did have twins, I'd give one away before I got attached to it.

Before tea I asked my father about his religious beliefs.

"I don't have any. Go ask your mother."

I found Mum in the kitchen.

"I do have some," she said, "but I don't want to influence you. You need to make up your own mind on that sort of thing."

I could see now I'd fit in and started looking forward to being in the 'religious exclusion' class.

WEDNESDAY

There are thirteen of us in the exclusion group. My joke about thirteen at the Last Supper was not appreciated, except by Lori. There's a painting of Jesus and the twelve disciples in her parents' bedroom.

I thought the Iranian Bahai in Year Three and the Kiwi-born Bahai kid in Year Four would be among us, but Rowan said they believe in religious tolerance. For them, any world religion, Hindu, Buddhism, Islam, Judaism or Christianity is fine. So they're not here with us. Their loss, I say.

When I was asked what my beliefs were I explained I was expelled from religious education because I'm argumentative and disobedient.

Eli Jacobson smiled and nodded. "This school needs more dissidents like you." (Must look that word up.)

He went on, "So what did you say to the Bible in Schools lady that got you sent to the Principal's office?"

I admit I did exaggerate, but not much. Finally, I think, I've found my tribe.

The boys and I had a children's menu kind of tea. Aunt Helene came to pick up Mum and Dad for his birthday dinner, with Nana on board. I didn't even know she'd come down on the bus from Napier. Nana is staying with Aunt Julie and Uncle Pete and they're all meeting up at the RSA.

Mrs Milton asked why make such a fuss over a 32nd?

Napier Nana says she sometimes regrets living so far away from her three Gisborne-based children and her six grandchildren. The birthday of her youngest is as good an excuse as any for a family reunion. Why wait? Life is too short to not take every opportunity for making special memories.

I think Gran and Mum's side of the family are invited too, plus a couple of Dad's work mates. Gran would never miss an occasion to dine at her favourite RSA restaurant.

The kitchen table was crowded with cards that said 32 or over the hill. Mum made Dad open his present from Nana. Inside was a white cable knit jersey.

Mum agreed it looked good on him, but added, "White! That will have the life expectancy of a match."

"Oatmeal," Nana corrected.

"Nana, I'd love a cream jersey like that, but with a collar and a black speck running through. Then I'd have a matching set with my favourite black houndstooth."

Nana made Mum promise she'll hand-wash Dad's new jersey, not throw it at the machine. Duh! Mum lives in hand-knit land and there's nothing she doesn't know about washing woollens.

Just as well Mrs Milton was out of the room settling the boys for bed. When Nana asked her, Mum said the twins absolutely loved their new teddy bears. I nearly choked on my Krispie biscuit. Those bears are shoved in the bottom of their toy box. They'd prefer any licensed soft toy instead. Mum is good at lying to her mother-in-law.

Then it was my turn.

"Rosalyn, I was disappointed to miss seeing you on your return trip from camp, but I know all about car problems. I hope you had a good time?"

I held Monkey closer and nodded. I knew my cheeks were pink. Aunt Helene frowned at me and began telling them how she drove like the clappers through Napier in the middle of the night to make up for time lost. At dinner Uncle Pete will probably ask awkward questions about her car. He's a mechanic.

If Aunt is thirty-nine and still lying to her mother, what hope is there for me?

I was going to stay awake to see how drunk they were when they came home. Drunk people are sometimes funny. Just as well Aunt Helene is behind the wheel. She won't drink even one glass of wine when she's driving.

I did get up at 12.20. Mrs Milton was in the lazy-boy with her mouth wide open and snoring loud as. I drank some milk straight out of the bottle, but left no evidence. I got tired of sitting up in bed waiting and fell asleep soon after.

THURSDAY

My parents shouldn't go to work today. They're like zombies. That's what drinking does to ageing bodies.

"Happy birthday, Dad."

I handed over his present, a box made of balsa wood and plywood. Not that well-made. It was hard to hold in the vice until the glue set, but the thought was there. He must've liked it. He cried. Inside were some pick-and-mix pineapple lumps.

"I can't face them now, Rosalyn, but thank you. I'll try one or two at smoko."

He must have noticed I was disappointed, and popped one in his mouth and passed another to Mum. They crunched them up, but I did think at one point they might be about to throw-up. They weren't interested in reading the paper. Too busy dividing up the Panadol to get them through a work day.

It's been a week since my letter to the editor was printed. I wanted to see if anyone had replied to it, so I folded that section up and shoved it in my bag. Not that the olds noticed. At interval Kirstie and I read the letters. There was one from a Captain Holloway.

"I wish to correct a misconception. It is not the Salvation Army's policy to remove items and exchange them for clean replacements unless asked to do so. We recognise and respect the right of the individual. The person who disposed of Desmond Burton's clothing did not in any way represent the Gisborne Branch of the Salvation Army."

The next one was signed E.J.

"I would like to point out to Ross Bovary that those of us who have been around these parts for more than ten years are aware of the long history between the townspeople and Desmond Burton. It is inaccurate and unfair to accuse the good people of Gisborne of neglecting this unfortunate man. Many attempts both in the past and present have been made to help him. He simply refuses such help.

"Ross Bovary obviously has a caring community conscience, but has much to learn to become an investigative journalist. Especially on this sensitive local topic. Some research before writing is a must before he – or she? – she puts pen to paper."

That she bit was a dead giveaway that made my heart jump.

"E.J must stand for Esmé Jondell," Kirstie confirmed.

"So she knows I'm Ross Bovary?"

"Obviously."

Aunt Helene had already read Mum's letter. She said exactly the same as Dad over the chocolate incident, when I refused to answer to Rosalyn.

"Your mother has called your bluff, Roz. Or should I call you Mr Bovary?"

We were still laughing when Sarah came into the room.

"What's so funny?"Aunt reached over and ruffled my hair. I'd never seen her look so like Dad.

"Oh, an old family joke, eh, Roz?"

FRIDAY

This is the last day for the inspectors. Noel Perkins must be relieved. I bet he can't wait to go back to putting his hand down his pants. When she heard me say this, Mum explained the inspectors are there to check on the teachers, not the pupils.

Mr Morrissey was nervous when he saw me talking to the inspector at lunchtime. Then Mr Collinson came right up to us and said, "A moment of your time, if I may Mrs Smithers.

Oh, I see you've met our budding young writer, Rosalyn Jondell. No doubt she's mentioned the scholarship we arranged. Attended the Regional Junior Writers camp last school holidays. Youngest member too I must add. A credit to our school. Yes, a credit to our school."

We hadn't even mentioned anything about school or writing. Mrs Smithers and I were bonding and networking. I had admired her suit, a neat navy blue today, and her haircut.

I asked who does her hair and she told me the name of some posh salon in Parnell. I'm going to tell Mum I want a haircut exactly like the inspector's.

SATURDAY

Kirstie's coming with us on the bus today, but she's not allowed to bring Jimmy. She has money for bus-fare and lunch at the diner. We've both promised to keep a close eye on the twins and not get distracted by each other's company.

Every Saturday when we go to meet Mum, the olds make me promise not to go anywhere near Desmond Burton. But at least my parents can see the sense in training up someone else to help with the boys. When I'm gone they'll have to pay Kirstie, of course, but we all know she'll do a good job.

I'll probably be in Bangladesh researching my Rhamat story. Or I might have won a scholarship to America where I can wear jeans to school. Anyway, Desmond wasn't under the bridge. He's in hospital. Again. I'm surprised my parents drink when they've both known about him for so long. Can't they can see the harm alcohol does to a person?

We watched old re-runs of Pukemanu on TV. Maybe I'll be an actor like Ginette McDonald or a television presenter like Brian Edwards.

SUNDAY

Desmond Burton was brain-dead and now they've turned off his life support. We heard it on the radio this morning. I got out my file headed with his name and wrote on it Deceased, and today's date. In that manila envelope are the newspaper articles and letters, including mine.

When I'm eighteen, I'll still write Desmond Burton's story. By then I expect there'll be another alcoholic to interview living under the bridge. His death has started me thinking about lots of things and I'm kind of sad in a funny sort of way.

Kirstie and I sat under the railway bridge, about a half mile from home and ate a half packet of Krispie biscuits she'd flogged from her house.

"Kirstie, isn't it weird my name's Jondell. If I was found dead and my body couldn't be identified, the tag on my toe would say John Doe. Nearly the same."

"No, it isn't," argued Kirstie, "it's not that close at all. Especially as you're a girl and you'd be Jane Doe, not John Doe."

"Depends. If Ross Jondell, in steel-capped boots, was involved in a stadium collapse, and a steel girder completely squashed his head while he was setting up sound and lighting equipment for a rock band, then I'd be a John Doe."

I leaned over and nicked the last biscuit.

"But if Roz Jondell in her smart jacket and short skirt got caught in a New York media office towering inferno and her face was burnt off, then I'd be a Jane Doe."

I wiped the crumbs off my mouth.

"Hey, maybe I do have confused identity just like Madame Bovary says."

Kirstie snorted. "You're confused all right if you think they won't notice the difference between a girl and a boy. And it's not a confused identity. Sounds to me like you've got an interchangeable persona."

"A what?"

"It happens when your soul hasn't transitioned

properly."

Kirstie has strong beliefs about re-incarnation. She's seen her own organs in various jars when she was the forgotten female pharaoh, Hatshepsut. No wonder she knows so much about ancient Egyptian burial rituals.

"I don't believe you come back as any sort of creature, Kirstie, or as a human, either. The world population is bigger now so the maths don't add up."

"But some souls are new, Roz. Here for the first time. You can't rely on maths for that."

"You'd better tell Mr Morrissey there's something maths is no use for. And my Dad. And Matt."

We giggled and stopped arguing about it. We talked instead about being buried alive. Kirstie said that in the old days a hole was drilled into coffins for a length of string to go through. This string was wound around the dead person's finger and attached to a bell in the cemetery.

If you awoke in your coffin, you rang the bell and someone would come and dig you up.

"That must be where the saying, For whom the bell tolls, comes from," I exclaimed.

"No, silly. If you're buried in a church cemetery, the church bells are rung the number of years you lived."

"Kirstie," I warned her, "no one likes a show-off. And if you don't watch out, Kirstie, you're going to turn into Miss Downes."

That shut her up until she murmured, "Mavis," then louder, "Mavis, darling."

We started giggling again.

"I suppose believing in an afterlife or even in reincarnation could be a comfort," I said. "You'd meet up with anyone you loved who'd died before you."

"What about the Undead?"

The evening sky was darkening and Kirstie shivered.

"What, vampires?"

"Yes. You must drive a stake through a vampire's heart to kill him."

"No," I scoffed. "That also comes from the fear of being buried alive before doctors had stethoscopes to detect a heartbeat. Sometimes when a coffin is dug up and opened, they've found scratches on the inside of the lid. So they asked for a stake through the heart because they didn't want to wake up and find they'd been put ten feet under."

By now it was dark and we started home. Every shadow had us jumping in terror. If I'd been late, I'd have been in big trouble, but I got through the door with four minutes to spare. Whew!

MONDAY

Mum says she has a friend at work who is a hairdresser. I shook my head.

"No, Mum. The inspector's hairstyle is unique and complicated in design. We need the kind of professional stylist you won't find in Gisborne."

"It's a basic bob, Rosalyn. Short at the back, long on the sides. The bob has been around since the flapper years of the 1920s. It became popular again in the 1960s and early 70s. I had one myself when I was eighteen."

She got up and we began clearing the dishes.

"And if you brush your hair properly every day for a week – one hundred strokes, no less! – I will see what I can arrange."

TUESDAY

My arm's worn out from all that brushing. When I asked

Jennifer if my hair looks different. She said, "Not much" and "Turn around."

"Yeah. You've brushed it at the back for a change and there's no knots in it."

WEDNESDAY

Mum showed me an old scrapbook from the 1920s. I couldn't believe it. Nearly all the actresses in it had the same hairstyle as the inspector's.

THURSDAY

He's been buried, but there's going to be a memorial service for Desmond Burton down by his bridge on Saturday afternoon at 2pm.

The Mayor is to lead it, along with the three social service providers. Mum wanted to go, and that surprised me, and I was surprised again when. Dad said, "Why not? Yes, let's go."

We talked about Colleen McCulloch at writers' group tonight, the Australian who wrote The Thorn Birds. She got thirteen million for that. Thirteen million!

Her photo was on the back cover and her hair was not professionally styled at all. That gives me hope. If she can land thirteen million when she doesn't give a toss about dressing for success, what should I be aiming for?

FRIDAY

Gran's also going to Desmond Burton's memorial. Mum asked her mother if she wants a lift, but she's shuffling on to the community van with the other old folk.

"Seems everyone and their dog is going, Esmé."

"Dad, it's not polite to talk about your mother in law like that."

My cousins Ralph and Jerrold are coming with us. The twins will spend the afternoon with Aunt Julie and

Jordan, who's also five. The five Jays I call them because even Uncle Trevor has a Joseph. What is it with the Jondell family? Only Ralph and me don't have a name beginning with J.

Uncle Pete dropped out. "Got no time for random funerals," he said. "Too many cars breaking down. I've got too much work on."

"Mum, I'd better write a few words for Desmond Burton's memorial in case I'm asked to speak."

Mum smiled, raised her eyebrows, and turned to Dad, who shrugged.

"If she wants to, why not? It'll keep her out of our hair if nothing more."

The thing is the cousins are camping overnight at ours after the memorial service. Aunt Julie and Uncle Pete are going out. Probably drinking. Hasn't anyone learnt from Desmond Burton's mistakes?

The sleeping arrangements will be Jerrold and Ralph, who's only one week younger than me, topping and tailing in my bed. I can either share a high bunk with the five-year-olds, put a mattress on their floor, or kip in with Mum and Dad. I think I will see what Kirstie's up to.

At school before bell rings. Can't stay at Kirstie's. They are settling a new boarder. There's too many at Lori's already. I worry about her. She thinks sleeping in a room with three five-year-olds is completely normal. Jennifer and Isobel's parents consider me a bad influence for some reason.

But I'm in luck. Macey Liddicott has always wanted me on a Saturday sleepover at hers, even after my Dad so rudely sent her packing that day we were on home detention.

I told my parents about the invitation tonight. They'll

phone Macey's mother. I hope they're not prejudiced by her looks. It's not Mrs Liddicott's fault she's such an old hag with no teeth and three fingers missing from her right hand.

SATURDAY

Just as well we got there early to park. The Mayor was already on the Band Rotunda. We set out our rug before the crowds arrived to get a good view up front.

I'm glad we swapped our twins for two older boys who don't need taking to toilet every fifteen minutes. The community van arrived with the pensioners and Gran and her pals shuffled to the reserved chairs set out for them. The Mayor's speech made some of them cry.

"Rosalyn, show some respect," Mum hissed. "Stop rustling that paper. Put it away."

There were other speakers from the Salvation Army, St Vincent De Paul, and I think the other was the Red Cross. Then the MC said, "And now we call upon someone who knew Desmond for most of his life, his neighbour, Mrs Coleman."

I gasped. Someone was helping my grandmother up onto the Band Rotunda. The Mayor brought out a chair for her, but she didn't sit down. She stood behind it with her hands on the back.

"Desmond was a good boy who lived directly across the road from me. He went out of his way to help his neighbours, especially the widows and the old. He did yard-work, cleaned windows, and he never asked for money."

She paused to blow her nose.

"Money was tight after my dear husband died. Once Desmond brought over two rabbits he'd shot when my family had no meat for the week. He was only fifteen when he re-made a trike for my daughter Esmé's seventh birthday. He repaired and rebuilt many toys for my children and others."

Mum was sniffing now. I had no idea she'd known him when she was younger than me. Desmond was nowhere near the age I had imagined. That's what drinking and rough living does to someone. Why, he was only Aunt Helene's age. Now Mum was crying and Dad held her hand.

After Gran went back to her seat, Captain Holloway of the Salvation Army spoke on how they'd tried to help Desmond.

He seemed to be looking straight at me when he said, "I'd like that Bovary bloke to retract his claims about an uncaring community now."

A security guard stopped me before I reached the steps. "Please go and sit down, little girl."

I dodged past him and shouted to the party up on the Band Rotunda and waved my papers. "I am that Bovary bloke. I want to answer that. I wish to speak."

The Mayor motioned to climb up and handed the microphone. I hardly needed my notes.

"I am going to be a writer when I grow up and I was going to interview Desmond Burton first. He has already taught me heaps."

I ticked them off on my fingers.

"That a mortgage is better than renting or being homeless. That not being able to get a good job limits your choices. That it's better to be a boring old teetotaller than a drinker who's sick, unhappy or dead."

I waved to Aunt Helene.

"I'll always be a sober driver, Aunt, I promise, and I'll take anyone's keys who isn't and hide them."

That wasn't supposed to be funny. Don't people know they shouldn't laugh at funerals?

"Thank you, Desmond. You put me off becoming an alcoholic when I'm grown up. I'm sure you've put others off destroying their brain cells."

The sobbing woman behind Ralph caught my eye and nodded. I hope my parents got the message too. I had lots more to say, but the Mayor took the mike off me.

"Thank you, miss or should I say mister?"

There were more laughs from the crowd. He handed me a bucket with a slot in the cover labelled Desmond Burton Memorial Seat Fund.

"This young lady is coming down to collect from you and I know you will be generous."

They were. The bucket was almost too heavy to carry by the time I handed it back to him. The Mayor lifted it up and jingled the coins.

"Great work, Ross Bovary. Off you go."

As I walked back to my own space on the family rug, someone called out, "Ross Bovary turned out to be a heck of a lot shorter than I expected. Don't think I'll punch his nose now." The woman who'd been crying shouted, "Who'd have guessed it was just a little girl?"

Others joined in.

"Only nine! That explains the ignorance."

"Not ignorant but innocent, bless her wee cotton socks."

(I was wearing woollen work socks if he'd looked.)

Then the Mayor explained what my letter was about for those who don't read the paper and weren't in the know. There were other comments as we walked to the car.

"What a brave girl."

"Your brothers should be proud."

I stopped, "I do have bothers, but these aren't them."

"I'm her cousin," Jerrold shouted, "and she's the coolest cousin on the planet." (He's sweet as sometimes.)

Ralph walked ahead like he didn't want to know us.

Now it's nearly nine o'clock and I'm trying to sit up and write in a saggy bed. I don't know why Mrs Liddicott hasn't put a couple of planks of timber under the mattress or tightened the springs. I would have. What's the worst is the smell, though I should be used to that with Justin.

Dad walked me the four blocks here. Jerrold came, too, but Ralph stayed back at the house. I'm glad I brought my writing with me cos I don't trust him not to read it.

Dad carried my bag. "Have you got the kitchen sink in here, Rosalyn? It's only one night. A change of clothes, your PJs and a toothbrush should do it."

If he knew me better, he'd have added Monkey to the list. Or even my diary.

SUNDAY

I won't ever spend the night at Macey's again. Didn't mind that Dad stayed for a cup of tea. I knew he'd get from Macey's mother the gruesome story of how she lost her fingers to a tomahawk when she was a little girl chopping kindling for the family woodstove. Macey says it's her only claim to fame.

I couldn't sleep. I was scared. Macey hardly talked for ten minutes before she dropped off. Now I know why no-one wants a sleepover at Macey's. About midnight one of her big sisters was dropped off by her boyfriend. He revved his engine in the driveway while Mrs Liddicott screamed at him, "You better not make me a grandma at only 33!"

33! Honestly, I thought she was older than Napier Nana. She woke the neighbours and when they complained yelled bad language and threats. She didn't wake Macey though.

I wish I hadn't come here.

About two in the morning I had to go to the loo. I didn't want to leave the room. I wish I had topped and tailed with a five-year-old in a decent bunk. My bum nearly touched the floor in that saggy wire wove.

I woke up again and so did Macey when lights flashed outside the window. We ran down the hall. A bunch of teens sat round the kitchen table drinking and smoking with Macey's mother.

One had blood on his face. We got yelled at, too, and went back to bed. Macey was soon sleeping again, but I stayed awake and as soon as it was light enough I was off. I didn't want breakfast, I wanted to get out. Oh boy, was that bag heavy! The shoulder strap cut into me and I had to stop and change over every few steps.

Back home, no one was up and I knocked on the door for ages. When Mum finally opened it there was no, "Did you have a nice time, dear?" She grunted and went back down the hall.

I called after her, "You'll make a great zombie next Hallowe'en."

She flapped a hand at me and went into her room. My cousins were fast asleep in my bed and I couldn't care less. I grabbed the foam mattress, a pillow and a spare quilt, dragged a sheet over the mattress and threw myself down flat without even taking off my shoes. I don't remember anything else until lunch time.

MONDAY

I told Kirstie, Lori and Jennifer about the police turning up at Macey's, something I never mentioned at home. When the olds finally asked me how I got on I said, "I had a good time, thank you." Writing teaches you how to lie.

TUESDAY

Dad was complaining again. "I wouldn't speak to my dog the way Gary Marks speaks to his kids."

I reminded him he won't let us have a dog. He ignored me and Mum refilled his mug.

"Did you hear the Liddicott crowd in Huiarau Street have done a moonlight flit, Steve? If we'd known the cops were going to turn up on Saturday night, we'd have never let you go there, Rosalyn."

"You should have rung me,' said Dad. 'I'd have come and got you straight away."

I thought a moonlight flit was something old ladies play on the piano, but it isn't. ("That's the Moonlight Sonata, you twit," said Kirstie.)

A moonlight flit is about state housing tenants mainly taking off in the night leaving unpaid rent and bills behind. So Mum was right. Macey wasn't at school and her cubby cube was cleared of exercise books. I wonder if I will ever see her again? Perhaps I'll go to her funeral when we're old. I will keep an eye out for her under the Old Colonial Bridge.

It's been over a week now and I've been brushing my hair with one hundred strokes every day. I will start nagging Mum next Monday. By then it will be two weeks since she promised the upmarket hair style.

WEDNESDAY

Religious exclusion class. We're expected to do self-directed learning. I wrote a story about POLICE CARS IN THE NIGHT and then two letters. The one to Madame Bovary went in the bin, but the group dared me to deliver my letter to the Bible in Schools lady. I did.

THURSDAY.

I'm in trouble and Principal shook his head sadly as I walked into his office. This time he'd sent for me. A copy of my letter was on his desk. Our Bible lady went mental with it, especially the bit about God being female, instead of male. She Creates. The Creator that is, not the Bible lady.

"Rosalyn, along with this letter Mrs Jolly has handed in her notice. She's retiring."

"I don't think unpaid volunteers can retire, Mr Collinson. Can they?"

"Whatever you want to call it, she's left us and we'll have to find someone else. That makes work for us, Rosalyn, and time that might be better spent on teaching you some manners. Sadly, it's back to the dishes for you, and as you like writing letters so much please compose a one page letter of apology to Mrs Jolly and pretend you mean every word. Now go!"

Kirstie shook her head sadly too. "Was that wise, Roz?' They'll just march in yet another dullard to brainwash the sheep."

Rowan stood up for me.

"All the world religions have got that God is a man part wrong. The ancients worshipped goddesses first, because it's women who bring new life into the world. I wonder if Mr Collinson's ever thought about that?"

When I handed him my letter to the Bible lady, Mr Collinson read it through in silence, though his mouth twitched once or twice. He promised to post it to Mrs Jolly.

Before he dismissed me he said, "Keep up the writing practice, Ross Bovary. That name has a ring to it. Frankly, I like it. Many writers write under multiple names. You've already established a readership here. My advice is to use it. Use every opportunity you've got to speak your mind and speak up for others."

Who'd have guessed *he'd* be at Desmond Burton's memorial service with his wife and grand-children. Well, he was.

FRIDAY

I'm diminished with school. I thought Papa endured saggy camp stretchers in the trenches so we could enjoy free speech.

SATURDAY

Kirstie told me the word I was looking for is disillusioned. She is sort of right, but I'm diminished by being disillusioned. That's what I told her anyway.

"Roz, it's OK to admit to being wrong sometimes."

"I know, Kirstie, and I'll do it the very first time I am wrong."

Finally, a weekend to work on the carts.

SUNDAY

In two weeks I will be ten. Double figures at last!

The carts are done. Dad ended up doing most of the work.

"Don't worry, Rosalyn. You're doing well and soon enough you'll be making them all on your own."

"Thanks, Dad." I hugged him. "I'm thinking soapbox derby next. Do you know, Marcia told me that Americans call a cart a soapbox and there's been a race every year since 1934 with championships held in Ohio. I've asked Marcia to send me some instructions. I could make a fortune building them for the kids around here."

"You go for it, girl," said Dad, and he walked away, whistling.

Kirstie and I took the carts to the hill by the railway

tracks for trials. Then I put Justin in front of me, and Josh climbed in with Kirstie. Soon there was a crowd of kids wanting a turn.

"Next time we'll charge in lollies or cash," said Kirstie.

The brakes aren't flash, but with skill they work well enough. Especially if we lay down an age or weight restriction.

MONDAY

Valerie Dixon from the Perfect Six came over when I was eating my snack at interval. Kirstie and I were sitting on the forms outside the classrooms. Valerie asked me all sorts of questions about the Bible teacher. She suspects I'm behind Mrs Jolly leaving the school in tears last Wednesday.

Turns out Mrs Jolly's a friend of Valerie's mother. I answered carefully. I've watched enough TV news and old documentaries to know how dangerous brainwashed congregations can be. But it's not just Christian sects who brainwash their converts. Just look at all the teenage runaways who join the Moonies.

I've been taking care of my hair and was going to start nagging Mum, but didn't need to. Whew! When she came home she announced her hair stylist friend will come over after work on Wednesday. The twins are muscling in on my big moment and getting a trim as well.

Kirstie, Lori and Jennifer will be blown away. I won't say anything before even to them. I bet when I walk into the classroom, my new look will remind Mr Morrissey of the inspector.

TUESDAY

What is it between me and the Perfect Six lately? Today Victoria Allen came over. Said she watched me speak at

Desmond Burton's memorial service. She reckons now my hair is neat and tidy I should wear a stretchy headband – she called it a bandeau – like the rest of them.

I don't want to be like the rest of them. I'll show them that when I walk into class on Thursday morning. Can't wait to see the reaction from the writers group too. One more day.

WEDNESDAY

They have a temporary Bible in Schools teacher for our class. He looks so feeble I'm worried he might fall over. It's hard to keep my mouth shut about the hairstyle.

I'm home. Waiting for Mum. Waiting for her work pal. Waiting for reform by scissors.

THURSDAY

I do like my new hairstyle and Mum's friend even put some light and darker shades into it so it looks totally natural. I dressed sharp this morning. Wish I had a skirt like the inspector's. Instead I chose a mint-green pleated skirt with a plain cream shirt. Mum has tried hard to get the ink off the left sleeve.

It was difficult to choose between a fringe or a side parting. I don't want a fringe. It's high time I outgrew that childish look now I'm nearly ten.

But Mum reminded me I'm not good at hair maintenance and I'll soon forget to use clips to stop my hair falling into my eyes. What if that happens at the wrong time, like while I'm using the table-saw? Don't want to end up fingerless like Mrs. Liddicott.

Last year for a fringe though. Definitely. But everyone at school likes my hair style, especially the teachers. Even the Perfect Six are impressed, totally, though they're pretending not to be.

I wanted to tell Victoria Allen she could stick her bando somewhere rude, but I kept my dignity as Gisborne Gran would say. The Perfect Six didn't rush over to tell me how grown up and smart I look because they're jealous. That's all.

Now they can't get a hairstyle like mine without becoming a bunch of copycats. They're stuck with their stupid bando style forever. Ha ha ha.

FRIDAY

Hosing down again. Dripping wet raincoats. Teachers nagging us to stack our gumboots neatly. Corridors smelling like wet dog.

Josh and Justin had another crisis over their slippers. They both hate the light-blue ones Mum put in their schoolbags. So I've swapped my forest green for that pair. Now my toes are squished together. Gran has a habit of making pairs in the same colour, one light and one dark. When I asked her why she said, "It encourages the boys' individuality."

They shove everything they hate in the bottom of their toybox, along with Nana's teddy bears. In there are pale yellow, apple green, fawn and lilac slippers. I like all of those, but they're too small for me. Mum should drop them at the Red Cross thrift shop, only she doesn't want to start World War 3 if Gran should visit.

Napier Nana has the right idea. When she makes slippers or jerseys or anything for the twins, she makes them identical. Then Josh and Justin can like them or loathe them together.

Tomorrow's Guy Fawkes. I'm glad the rain stopped shortly after we got home from school. The backyard is full of puddles, but Dad says provided there's no more rain, our yard will have drained by then. I do like fireworks and a bonfire!

"Money going up in smoke," Dad calls it. That's his attitude. And Mum says exactly the same thing every year.

"What is it about Kiwis that we're so fascinated by some ancient attempt to blow up the British Parliament?"

We're lucky to have Guy Fawkes fall on a Saturday this year. My parents don't spend much on firecrackers, it's mainly sparklers and *one* sky rocket. Yes, one, and Dad thinks the day will come when sky rockets will be banned.

He says that's not a bad thing because some people can't be trusted to use them safely. He's building a stockpile so he can let one off somewhere safe like into the sea every year for the rest of his life.

Dad's got a new incinerator drum, so he punched a few more holes in the rusty old drum and let us use that.

"When my mother was a girl she and her friends went around the neighbourhood with a Guy Fawkes in a wheelbarrow calling out a penny for the guy."

That's how they raised funds to buy firecrackers in the olden days. A penny! When I told Kirstie she said, "What's that?" But thanks to Mum's stories and Matt Branson I know more than I'll ever need to know about the imperial currency system.

We made our guy by stuffing a pair of Dad's old overalls with crumpled newspaper. The head is the top part of a pantyhose padded with rags and a mask for a face. Our guy wears one of Dad's discarded work hats with Plimmers Plumbers written above the peak.

Kirstie, Lori, Jennifer, Isobel and I took our guy around in the cart. We're not asking for money. We're inviting neighbours to bring their fireworks and a pot luck contribution for tea at our place tomorrow night. We're getting excited about burning our guy and watching the rockets fly high.

SATURDAY

We didn't go into town to meet Mum. Instead Dad took us to the beach in Plimmers' van. I talked him into letting Kirstie come along to help load up the driftwood. Then he barked at us for sitting around building sandcastles and not helping him and the twins load the van.

List of arrivals at Guy Fawkes: Kirstie, Mrs Jarrett and Jimmy. No baby, thank goodness. Their Dad's home from the bush.

Aunt Helene and Sarah, the Sorrens, Isobel, Jennifer, Warner, Vinny. No baby Julia. Yippee! It's too dangerous for babies around fireworks although she will be welcome to come to our Guy Fawkes when she's a little bit older, of course. Mrs Milton and her old pal Mr Diver from across the road.

Rowan and her mother Wild-Wolf. Lori with two brothers, the twins' friends, one five and one six years old. Because of little brothers she can't stay late, but Mum says Josh and Justin can stay up until they fall asleep.

Food: Mum made three salads and Dad pre-boiled a stack of home-kill sage and onion sausages for the BBQ. Wild-Wolf brought Vegelinks, vegetarian sausages. She showed us a bit of her 'wild wolf soul' when Vinnie gobbled up half of them. Rowan should have warned her there'd be feral children here.

I don't know who brought the tasty avocado dip with carrot and celery sticks. More salads. More breadsticks. A selection of cheeses. Two coconuts and a pineapple. The basket of scones wrapped in a tea-towel with a pot of blackberry jam was provided by Mrs Milton. Only the old people ate these.

Oh, Dad's lighting the fire.

SUNDAY

When I got up this morning, there were four people sleeping on our porch surrounded by empty bottles and overflowing paua shell ashtrays. The incinerator smouldered and our guy was a melted mess of twisted material.

Mrs Milton wandered over from next door in her dressing gown. She started pouring coffee into mugs from one of the two thermos flasks she brought with her. Nobody wanted her re-heated scones.

The Sorrens went home early in the evening after Warner's accident with the coconut.

"Don't indulge him by mentioning it," said Mum. "At thirteen he's old enough to know better. The boy was merely attention seeking and the entire incident too stupid for words."

Aunt Helene agreed. "Warner Sorren has the IQ of a wombat."

I'm hoping his sisters won't be banned from coming over. It's not their fault they've got a moron for a brother.

MONDAY

Today it was all over our school about Warner getting injured below the belt with a hammer. Just as well both him and Vinny go to Central Intermediate.

I gathered up a maximum number for a first-hand account from Kirstie. She didn't want to be forced to repeat it and we knew who we could rely on to spread it around.

"Why ever would he put the coconut down his pants and ask his brother to smash it with the hammer?"

Yes, Victoria Allen, that's the $64,000,000 question and it's still unanswered.

Kirstie kept them spellbound from start to finish. The backdrop of fireworks and an exploding guy lighting up the sky. (We'd laced him with crackers.) She had Warner's blood spilling down – the coconut water was dark in the shadows – and Warner's screams of pain and terror. The shrill siren of an ambulance racing through the city streets.

Kirstie managed to make our Guy Fawkes' Night an event you'd be sorry to have missed. Warner was the only casualty: no fire, no other injuries. And Kirstie managed to make him sound like some brave fallen hero. His fans wanted to bike to the hospital and cheer him up. What she didn't say was he wouldn't be there. He was sent home straight after treatment and biked to school this morning with something Mum called an iced sanitary pad shoved down his uniform shorts to help with the bruising.

Warner was embarrassed when that got out. The school nurse at Central Intermediate knew all about his injury and organised additional ice to get him through that day and the next.

TUESDAY

Finally, we have a booking for my room. I'm glad it's not this weekend because it's my birthday. The paying guests arrive the weekend after.

"Two men," said Mum. "They'll be sharing."

I stared at her. "Grown men? How weird."

"It's not weird at all, Rosalyn," she snapped. "Some men don't mind sharing and these two have been friends for some time." Then she winked at Dad, and went on, "Besides, they're coming for an art exhibition, aren't they,

Steve. They're *artists*, Rosalyn."

As if that explained why they don't mind topping and tailing.

"Did you ever want to share a bed with a friend, Dad?"

He laughed. "Once, waiting for a new house, Trevor and I did exactly that." Uncle Trevor is eleven years older than Dad.

"Your aunts, Julie and Helene, were forced to share the only other room. Nana's."

"I'd hate to share with a snoring old woman, wouldn't you, Mum?"

"I'll have you know, young lady, she wasn't always old. My mother-in-law was an attractive young woman in her day."

Dad sighed. "The arrogance of youth, eh, Esmé? Rosalyn, in about forty years karma will catch up with you."

"49? No. I don't want to live that long."

Mum laughed. "You might feel differently about that when you're 48, my girl."

WEDNESDAY

I'm not entirely sure Dad is happy with our house guests' sleeping arrangements. I heard them arguing about it after they thought we were asleep. As usual. Mum thinks it's absolutely fine. She's probably going to offer a discount for inconvenience.

The last thing I heard Dad say was, "Oh well, Esmé. Someone round here is going to take their money. Might as well be us."\

Mum had better buy in some decent food to make a good impression. Eggs Benedict, perhaps. I'm sure Sarah can provide a recipe. And something like salmon and asparagus for lunch. Aunt Helene says food that goes together well goes down well.

I like salmon and asparagus, especially with cheese sauce. But then everyone tells me I have sophisticated tastes for my age. And that's what Sarah provided for tea the first night I met her – I'd never even tasted salmon or asparagus before that.

I wish I could film the twins' faces though when they see asparagus on their plates. They *hate* it.

THURSDAY

If the men who are staying are artists, I might ask who'd like to illustrate Rhamat of Bangladesh. I can afford $5. Or they can wait until it's a bestseller or a TV series and share some of the profit.

Now that I'm older, I need to develop a sense of business. I don't want to get ripped off. Kirstie says that happens too often to creatives like me.

At writers' group tonight I told them I'll be ten tomorrow. We talked about Christopher Robin Milne. It's hard to believe that little boy in the Hundred Acre Wood grew up and got old. I looked him up; he was born in 1920.

That makes the real Christopher Robin 57 now. I hope I don't live long enough to be that ancient, and all grey and wrinkled.

FRIDAY

Finally it's my birthday. Ten today. Ten. Ten. Ten.

I pretended to sleep in so they could get ready to shower me with presents. When no one did, I had to ask.

"Go on then," said Mum. "You can open this parcel from Nana. You'll have to wait until your party this afternoon to open the others."

I ripped off the candy-striped wrapping paper. Inside was the cream cable knit jersey exactly like Dad's, except for the collar and the black specks running through the wool.

When I put it on, Mum patted the collar into place and did up its three top buttons. I'm not planning on taking it off any time soon. It makes me feel so grown up.

When I got home after school, the table was loaded with party food for my birthday tea. Mum had made me a mouse cake. (I wanted a rat in memory of Desmond Burton) Its nose and whiskers were made of liquorice and its body was smothered in cream royal icing.

Kirstie gave me a Dragon album. Cool as. Lori's present was a hair brush, not exactly new but she'd managed to get most of the hair out. From Isobel I got a pencil case filled to overflowing with biros and pencils from nearly every business in town.

Then Jennifer handed me a crumpled paper bag.

"I got it from the Red Cross thrift shop."

I pulled out a green knitted hat with a kiwi on the front. Best hat ever!

"Thanks, Jennifer!"

She laughed. "I paid for it with some of my chook money."

"Now that's something you won't grow out of in a hurry, Rosalyn!" said Mum.

She's always complaining that I grow out of my clothes before they're worn out. She should have had twin girls after me!

"While we're on the subject of clothes…"

Sarah handed me a pink parcel tied in blue ribbon. I tore it open and there was my most favourite top in the whole wide world. Pale orange checked with darker orange.

"Oh, thank you," I blurted out. "How did you know I liked this so much?"

"I saw you eyeing it up way back in August that day we went into Farmers Department store. I got you the next size up though. Hope it fits."

She took it off me and measured it against my back. Aunt Helene nudged Mum.

"Plenty of room for growth there, eh, Esmé?"

"Yes," Mum agreed. "Now, hold on, Rosalyn. There's one thing more."

And she handed me another parcel. Inside was a jacket with matching skirt and trousers and a pure linen shirt. Everything went together and fitted me perfectly. When I opened it, I hugged her hard.

"However did you guess I wanted a suit like that?"

"Drip, drip, drip," she said. "You ever hear of water wearing away stone, Rosalyn."

I went a bit pink when they all started laughing. I thought that was the last thing, and it had already turned out to be a fab birthday. Then Dad and Aunt Helene slipped outside and came back wheeling in something big on Dad's handcart hidden under a tarpaulin.

When I pulled it off there was an old writing desk in blond oak, beautifully restored.

Dad handed me the key.

"Now you can stop obsessing about anyone reading your diary."

I was nearly crying. Mum whispered that Aunt Helene and she had bought the desk and Dad had been secretly working on it for weeks. I couldn't stop hugging them one by one.

"Thank you. Thank you. Thank you."

Inside one compartment was a card with a picture of a lone figure rowing up a peaceful river with fields with wildflowers and lush paddocks both sides. I read what

was written inside.
   "May all your dreams come true, Ross/Roz."
   The card was signed Madame Bovary.

JACK JONDELL
GISBORNE, TUESDAY 2017

Nan stood in the doorway, hands on hips.

"Sorry to interrupt your reverie, Jack!" Then she tapped her watch and pointed to the time.

"I don't know if you realise, but it's twenty to four already. Your sister is due home in about twenty minutes."

Why can't Nan say it's 3.40 like everyone else?

"I need to lock up now, and we're cutting time a bit short. I'll write you another note for school. Let's say Friday."

I held up the journal and waved it at her.

"But I've finished reading it, Nan."

"What – the entire thing? Surely not."

I grinned. You don't often get a chance to surprise Nan Helene.

"Yep." I passed the journal over.

"Any questions?"

"Yeah. Did Grandma Rosalyn ever find out about Madame Bovary?"

Nan pursed her lips and thought for a minute.

"I'm not entirely sure about that, Jack. There's so much we don't know. That we may never know. Now you must solemnly promise me, Jack, not to breathe a word. You can imagine how sensitive the subject of Rosalyn is."

She sighed heavily.

"Hinemarama's not ready, and I've had to face the

painful fact that your mother may never be. I've been patient so long that I've grown tired of waiting."

She sat down, the journal held between her hands.

"Yet I strongly feel that a full forty years after she began writing Rosalyn would want her diary to be read. She has a right to be heard; to live on through the memories of her children and grandchildren."

I nodded my head. I agreed with her absolutely.

"Nan, this is our whakapapa. Mum and Hine and me wouldn't exist if it wasn't for Rosalyn, eh?"

"Quite right, Jack. I can tell you now that *lost without trace* is the worst way to lose a child. If one goes missing at sea, there'd be no closure there, either, but at least you can presume they drowned."

I went and stood before her.

"But Rosalyn's alive, Nan. I met her. She even called me Hamiora and Sam. That means she knows my name, eh?"

Then I told Nan about that dream I had the night before I started reading Rosalyn's diary.

Nan listened carefully, then she sighed again and said, "You may well be right, Jack. One can only live in hope."

"Nan, I want to go on that Lost and Found show."

"We will talk about that at some later stage, Jack, I promise. Now as quick as you can, out of that filthy baseball jersey and those jeans and on with your school uniform. On your bike now, and it would help if you can manage to return a bit puffed. Come back when you see the school bus."

Nan reached over and ruffled my hair.

"You know something, my lad? Your grandmother Rosalyn would be proud if she could see you now."

"She can, Nan. She can."

She shook her head and got up to lock the journal in the

writing desk. She followed me out and closed the door behind her.

"Off you go, now, Jack! Hurry. We'll get to all this later."

Yeah, right. We all know what grown-ups are like. But no time to worry about that now. Like a good boy, I did exactly as I was told, then rode off on my bike, whistling.

The End

Loved the Book?

Please leave a review.

https://www.amazon.com/Robin-Lee-Robinson

ABOUT THE AUTHOR

Robin Lee-Robinson lives now in the Eastern Bay of Plenty where she's a trustee for the 1926 Opotiki De Luxe theatre and writes reviews of films shown there for the local newspaper.

This is her first Young Adult novel, planned as a series, but she has also published *In Salting the Gravy*, the memoir of a marriage, and *Talkback Toast: a Reminiscence of Radio Pacific*, where she worked as a producer. This featured Trevor Watson, one of their oldest listeners, and contributions from staff and audience.

A long-term member of Tauranga Writers, she regularly contributes to *Byline*, and has written presentations, talks and performance skits for a number of occasions, literary and historical.

Leisure interests include kayaking, tree-pruning and fishing.

Book 2 - Journal of a Junior Writer

In this sequel to *Diary of a Kiwi Kid*, Jack Jondell – whose koro named him Hamiora – is handed yet another journal by Rosalyn, from his missing grandma's locked writing desk. With his twin sister, mother and Nanny Sarah away up in Tokomaru Bay, Nan Helene allows Jack to stay home from school to secretly read Rosalyn's journal. They have no sooner waved goodbye to the whanau when she passes it over.
"Jack," she says, "you are to read no farther than to where I've marked. Then skip to Rosalyn's works in progress stapled to the back cover." This Gisborne boy is so intent on solving the mystery of Rosalyn's disappearance in Bangladesh that he reads more than he should. He is determined to uncover clues to find her, alive or dead. Engrossed in this mystery of the past, time flies by...

Book 3 - Trials & Tribulations
of a Troubled Teen

In the story that began with *Diary of a Kiwi Kid*, Jack
Jondell – whose koro named him Hamiora – is handed yet
another diary from the locked writing desk of Rosalyn,
his long-lost grandma. While his sister, mother and
Nanny Sarah are away competing at a national kapa haka
festival, Nan Helene allows Jack to stay home from school
to read Rosalyn's last journal. He soon discovers this is
no primary schoolkid's outpourings like before. Jack has
been trusted with the biggest family secret ever. So what
exactly is the mystery behind Rosalyn's disappearance
from a Bangladesh slum 32 years ago? Everyone thinks
she is probably dead. Jack believes, fervently, that she is
alive. In Trials and Tribulations of a Talented Teen, the
mystery of Jack's grandmother is finally revealed ...

Salting the Gravy

ROBIN LEE - ROBINSON

Talkback Toast is written from two perspectives, that of a young woman producing husband Barry Crump's popular Bush Telegraph show, and Trevor, a caller who has stuck with radio, and like many of his generation, has witnessed the beginning of a brand new media. It includes the pioneer era and contains familiar names like Aunt Daisy, Uncle Scrim and Selwyn Toogood. The historical portion ends with Gordon Dryden, founder of Radio Pacific. It includes working in talkback in the early 1980's, and also covers the authpr's life with Barry Crump, much of it in bush settings, prior to and following their short stint in radio. The final portion contains submissions from the public and radio staff, beginning with a story written by Merv Smith who still hosts a radio show on Sunday morning through Radio BSport.

Talkback Toast

This is Robin Lee-Robinson's account of her 12-year marriage to Barry Crump. It's about her life and is the story of the man behind the myth; it is also about dealing with domestic abuse.

CONTACT

146

Facebook: https://www.facebook.com/
robin.leerobinson.9

Email: robinleerobinson@gmail.com

ACKNOWLEDGEMENTS

Grateful thanks to Angela Curtis for dragging this dinosaur kicking and screaming into the eBook era, and for assisting me with all things technical.

And to Jenny Argante, who ran the notion of eBooks past my consciousness many years ago in the first place. For being my ever-patient editor, and a mentor in so many aspects of producing a book.